MERCIFUL

REDEMPTION

A novel by

Tedla F. Bedada

MERCIFUL REDEMPTION
by Tedla F. Bedada

Published in the United States of America by Tedla F. Bedada
  • injewetrust@yahoo.com

This book is a work of fiction. Names, characters, businesses, places, events, locales, and incidents are either the products of the author's imagination or used fictiously. All characters are fictional, and any similarity to people living or dead, or actual events is purely coincidental.

Scripture taken from the New King James Version®. Copyright © 1982 by Thmas Nelson. Used by permission. All rights reserved.

All other Scriptures taken from the Holy Bible, New International Version®, NIV®. Copyright © 1973, 1978, 1984, 2011 by Biblica, Inc.™ Used by permission of Zondervan. All rights reserved worldwide. www.zondervan.com The "NIV" and "New International Version" are trademarks registered in the United States Patent and Trademark Office by Biblica, Inc.™

International Standard Book Number: 978-0-578-51901-2

Printed in the United States of America

Cover design, interior design and page layout by Tedla F. Bedada.

DEDICATION

This book is dedicated with love and affection to my beloved readers, who have lost faith or hope and have simply given up on life or their dreams. May you find the true meaning of hope and redemption that the loving God has for your life through His son, Jesus Christ.

EPIGRAPH

We can make this world a better place out of desperation, but we cannot make this world a better place out of perfection. A perfect world awaits with our Lord Jesus Christ, the coming King.

Tedla F. Bedada

ACKNOWLEDGMENT

This project would not have been possible without the support of my beloved family. I am so grateful to my parents, my sister, and my brothers who have provided me extensive personal and professional guidance and who have been unending inspiration and taught me a great deal about life in general. I am truly blessed and thankful to God to have such a wonderful family and role model.

I would like to include a special note of thanks to my editor, Jannette Fuller who gave her best to the project and who prayed and encouraged me throughout the entire process.

Most of all I thank my Lord Jesus Christ for His gift of redemption, grace and mercy in my life. It is my prayer that He blesses this work and uses for His good purpose in the lives of my beloved readers. Any good wisdom in this book comes from Him alone.

CHAPTER 1

Ruth was in the living room, sitting in her old rocking chair. She stared outside the window, waiting for her daughter to return home with her fulfilled dream. Lydia had auditioned for a singing contest—that she was selected to be part of—to represent her school. But due to her difficult health condition, Ruth could not accompany her daughter.

Lydia left early in the morning, leaving her ill mother behind, hoping for a brighter future through her success. She made great progress, and lots of sacrifices, to make it to the state contest that would give her a chance to go for the National Singing Contest. When Lydia left home, there was no doubt in her mind that it was her day to shine, showing the judges, the audience, and her mother, that she had what it took to be a young star.

Ruth was still rocking in her chair, waiting for her daughter's phone call. The summer season had made the sky look as if it were early in the afternoon. If Ruth had not looked at the time on her phone, she wouldn't have realized it was already passed 4:00 p.m. Tired of waiting, Ruth dozed off.

After a while, the door opened and Lydia entered the house. Lydia was cautious to not wake her mother, but Ruth's eyes popped open when she heard movement around her. It wasn't hard for Ruth to notice her teenage daughter's nonverbal cue about her day. Ruth was desperate to ask Lydia what she had been up to along with wanting to know why she looked so sad. The creaking of Ruth's rocking chair echoed in the room as she got up, holding the armrests.

"Hi, Mom," greeted Lydia with shades of sadness that hovered over her face.

"Hi honey, is everything ok?" Ruth remained silent, trying to ease up Lydia's emotions, but she had a hard time when it came to her own. She was concerned due to her daughter's late arrival.

Lydia finished her contest on time, the time she had told her mother, but due to her lack of success, she decided to stay out for a while before she returned home.

Lydia refrained from responding right away, trying to hold on to her frustration. She wanted her mother to think she was ok. Putting her bag on the table, she avoided answering the toughest question in her entire life when her mother, once again, asked how she was.

Lydia strove to keep her feelings under control, knowing she could not avoid the question any longer.

"Everything is fine, Mom." Lydia's voice was dejected.

"Tell me, honey, what really happened," insisted Ruth, as she looked into her daughter's eyes.

"I said I'm ok," replied Lydia in a leave-me-alone kind of voice.

Ruth paused her adamant quest, giving her daughter a moment to reconcile her thoughts. She held onto Lydia's hand and said, "It's ok, honey."

Lydia's eyes filled with tears. "No. It's not, Mom. I didn't make it."

Ruth comforted her with a firm grip on her shoulders as she looked into her eyes.

"Mom, this is what I was hoping for, this was our only chance to get us out of this situation." Lydia burst into tears unable to hold on to her emotions.

Ruth clenched her teeth, trying to handle the pain she was feeling as well. "It's all right, honey, you will make it next time," she whispered into Lydia's ear. She cuddled her daughter and shed a few tears of her own as she soothed her with a gentle touch to the back.

"There's no other chance, Mom, this was the only one I'll ever get. But it's too late. I just wanna be able to be here for you, to provide for you." Lydia was refereeing to Ruth's critical health situation.

"No, it won't be too late, honey. You just began your journey, so don't allow this experience to hold you back. You are such a talented girl and I believe in you, Lydia."

Lydia looked her mom in the eyes. "Thanks, Mom."

Ruth smiled back as she wiped away the tears on her daughter's chin.

"Did you get something to eat?" asked Lydia.

"Yes I did, honey. Dinner's in the fridge."

"Thanks, Mom. But I'm not hungry right now." Lydia walked to her room with nothing else to say.

Lydia was living with her single mother in a very difficult condition. For about a year and a half, Ruth hasn't been able to work. She was diagnosed with a stage three pancreatic cancer that was progressing to stage four. The doctors said she had six months or less to live. They were surviving with government assistance

programs along with the generous support of Ruth's family and close friends.

Lydia worked full-time during the summer season, which turned into part-time once school had started, but her mother did not want her to work. Instead, she wanted Lydia to focus on her classes and to get good grades. Lydia tried everything she could to help her mother, looking at alternatives to extend her life. And then, she saw an opportunity. There was an announcement on her school bulletin board about a singing contest. It was her greatest hope that being a part of this could change her family's life, especially when it came to the treatments her mother desperately needed. She had convinced her mother the contest would not affect her classes and that she would be fine to participate.

It had been three weeks since Lydia started participating in the contest. Despair, however, had replaced her dream due to her inability of coping with the fast-paced circumstances that surrounded her life: her mother's health condition, the rigid work schedule, and the lack of close friends to cheer her up, other than her mom. She was overwhelmed and barely made it to the state contest, which was the second step before nationals—the final step of the contest. But Lydia was totally shattered when she didn't make it to the final stage.

Lydia sat on her bed, cutting her toe nails, when her cell phone rang. She grabbed the phone and checked who was calling—it was her childhood best friend, Abigail. But she decided not to answer. A message was left and Lydia listened: "Hey, Lydia, just wanna know how you've been. And uh, please give me a call when you get this message. Bye."

Weeks had passed since the two inseparable friends had met, making it unbearable to Lydia. Since the beginning, the singing contest had not been easy, even more so since she didn't have a friend who did not share her dream of becoming a star. It was ironic for Lydia to have such a friend, a best friend at that. For Abigail was born and raised in a Christian family and never accepted the idea of secularism. And because of that, she stood firm in her faith.

A while back, Abigail and Lydia had an argument, following Lydia's shared thoughts of her dream to Abigail—the idea of going for the singing contest. They lived closed to each other and attended the same high school, so they walked to school together, chatting on their way there, and on their way back. And this is what happened on the day when Lydia had shared her dream to Abigail as they walked back home.

"Hey Abby, I wanna tell you something," said Lydia excitedly.

"What is it?" Abigail looked equally excited to hear what Lydia had to say.

"Not trying to be conceited, but you know how you're always telling me what a great voice I have?"

Abigail nodded. "Uh-huh."

"And have you seen the singing contest posted on our school board?"

"Yeah."

"Well, I've been thinking about it."

"About what?" Abigail knew full-well what she was referring to, but denial and fear gripped her heart.

"About being a part of the contest."

"Uh...ok." Abigail took in a deep breath and then released it. "Don't get me wrong, you do have one of the most anointed voices I've ever heard, but every time I mentioned it, I was referring to using your voice to praise the Lord—not praising and glorifying this world." Abigail also mentioned one of Lydia's favorite songs as an example of singing the world's praises.

"You don't like listening to songs unless it's Christian, most of the time, right?"

"Well, not most of the time. I listen to Christian songs *all* the time."

"Right. Blah, blah, blah."

Abigail frowned, clearly hurt and offended by Lydia's response.

"Ok, I'm sorry. But as for me, I listen to both. Anyways, the contest begins in the next few days, and registration is already open."

Abigail nodded with a forced smile.

"I'm gonna go for it, and I hope you'll be there to back me up."

Abigail kept silent for a moment, thinking it would be a bad idea to give Lydia any positive signs.

"Abigail." Lydia paused to collect her thoughts. "I didn't even tell my mom 'cause I'm kind of scared she might not let me go."

"Uh...I don't think that's a smart idea either, Lydia. Sorry to say, but we have a very busy schedule right now: assignments, quizzes, and on top of that, we're gonna have final exams at the exact time of the contest, which is like in a couple of weeks." Abigail tried to justify her discouraging words. "Hope you don't mind, but why do you want to do this, Lydia?"

"Mind? Of course I mind!"

"Ok, ok. Just trying to understand your motive behind it."

"My motive?"

"Meaning, it may interfere with your classes and your grades. Finals are in the next two weeks and we have to prepare for college. Soon enough, and we'll be heading to our biggest chapter in life."

"Yeah, yeah, yeah. I got it. But the contest is offering a life-time opportunity, at least to the winner, and the top three finalists. Just wished the timing wasn't an issue. It begins the same time when we'll be finishing out the school year."

"It doesn't matter, Lydia. We only have another year left before college, and you have to understand that this is the harvesting season for the coming years. Last time I remember, we agreed to work toward that plan. If you want to be part of the contest, then you know you have to practice, which will get in the way of completing our assignments on time along with getting good grades. We won't be accepted into any college, or university, if we don't this. You even told me you have to retake an exam for one of your subjects to improve your final grade, remember? As your best friend, you need to focus on that more than anything else."

Quietness reigned between them for a while. Lydia struggled with Abigail's friendly advice and the decision she had to make about participating in the contest. An opportunity she believed that was not only timely, but one that could significantly change her life for the better. Even more so for her mother.

"I know you're so into it, but the timing is bad," said Abigail. "Plus, I'm just afraid it might affect your final grade. Please continue to think about it, ok?"

"Do me a favor, and forget about my grade." Lydia huffed. "Once I get done with my assignments, I think I'll be fine."

"I think you're being way too emotional right now. You need to think about what you're trying to do, before you just do it."

"I don't need to think about anything." Lydia was super upset. "I just, I just can't believe this, Abigail. There are other students who've already registered to join the contest. Why do you think I'm different from the rest of them? I thought you would be the greatest supporter concerning my dream."

"I will always support you and your dreams, Lydia. I don't know about the other students, or their plans about the contest, but I know you very well. And let me tell you something, those students may not have a good friend like you do. Sorry but I'm just being honest. They may not have a friend who tells them when they're right, or when they're wrong. But I believe God put us together to look after each other. So I have to say something whenever I see something wrong in you, including supporting a dream that can harm you."

Lydia stopped in her tracks and looked right into Abigail's eyes. "Are you serious right now? You know what, forget it. I should have never asked for your opinion about my business. I honestly thought you would love to hear what I had to say, or what I wanted to do." With that, Lydia stormed off, speed walking the rest of the way home.

CHAPTER 2

Abigail picked up her pace and caught up with Lydia. "I always love to hear what you have to say, but maybe this is not the right time, or the right thing to do. I mean, if you go in this direction, I don't think the outcome will be good."

"And why's that?"

"Because it might make you—"

Lydia clenched her jaw. "Famous, rich...maybe both?!"

"Seriously, if that's your answer," began Abigail, "it won't count for your eternal life."

"You know what...forget it." Lydia continued to walk in silence.

"How can you expect me to stand beside you when you're getting ready to make a poor decision, escorting yourself into darkness?"

Abigail trailed behind, but then she stopped when Lydia spun around to face her. Lydia's eyes were wide, her brows raised in shock. She was having a hard time understanding where Abigail was coming from.

"Lydia, the Bible says, 'What good will it be for someone to gain the whole world, yet lose their soul? Or what can anyone give in exchange for their soul?'"

"I don't believe this, and I don't need your advice anymore. I thought we were friends. And I thought we agreed *not* to argue about religion, to protect our friendship."

"I'm not trying to argue with you. And when it comes to our friendship, I value it more than you realize." Abigail's lip quivered with sadness and frustration. "I'm just trying to tell you the truth because I love you so much."

"Yeah, right. If you really cared, then you would support me about chasing my dream. But no matter what, I'm still gonna compete because my mom needs me." Lydia shook from the onslaught of negative emotions.

"My mom's health is declining and she hasn't been able to work, so it's up to me to do something to help her."

"Lydia, I...I'm really sorry about that. But why are you just now telling me this? You should have told me she was getting worse."

"'Cause unlike you, I was trying to be a good friend. You have your own family issues to deal with. And I didn't wanna add more stress to your life."

"I appreciate that, but still, you should have told me. I'm always here for you, and I'm always praying for you and your mom."

"But how? All you've done is crush my feelings about the contest. It's the complete opposite of being here for me."

"Again, I'm so sorry. But can we please not fight anymore?" Abigail tried to encourage Lydia by reciting certain Scriptures along with giving her more advice about her situation.

"So in other words, I need to be just like you—all righteous and perfect for God to fix my mom. To fix everything!"

"Seriously! How can you say that? You know I'm just trying to help, so stop twisting my words." Abigail closed her eyes and heaved a sigh. "You're more than a friend to me, you're like my sister. And you know that. All I'm saying, is please let someone from the church come and pray for your mom. I believe the Lord will heal her."

Lydia took off without saying a word, leaving her friend behind once again. It didn't take long for Abigail to catch up, though. They arrived at the crossroads and then parted ways to go home. But then Abigail called out with a plea, "Lydia, please think about what I said!"

School was out and summer break had started. Now that Lydia and Abigail had more time to help their families financially, including personal expenses, they obtained summer jobs. Besides their occasional arguments, the girls had never stayed apart for too long. But this summer was different. Abigail was attending a Bible study group at least twice a week while Lydia attended a local music and dance club. They did make the time to chat either by phone or in person. However, it was short-lived.

Days had passed since they last met, which would have been very odd if they had not argued again. Lydia was upset with Abigail because she still resisted her dream of reaching stardom. Then again, everything

Abigail predicted had been coming to pass: some of her grades were being affected as she practiced for the contest. It was so hard for Lydia to keep everything in balance. She was so concerned about not making it to college, which made her feel like a loser. Shame and guilt plagued her as well.

Abigail attempted to get Lydia to meet her in person, but none of her attempts had worked. For Lydia spent the last few days clearing her voice mail that Abigail had bombarded with back to back messages. Resorting to her last option, Abigail had taken the liberty to visit Lydia and her mother, but Lydia wasn't home that day—she was at work. So before Abigail left their house, she asked Ruth where she was working.

One day Abigail had decided to leave work early, so she could meet with Lydia. But before she entered Lydia's work place, she said a prayer:

Please, Lord, give me strength and peace. And please open Lydia's heart so she'll want to talk with me. In Jesus's name. Amen.

Abigail greeted one of the employees at the desk. "Hi, can I see Lydia please?"

"Yeah"—the employee pointed toward Lydia—"she's right there."

"Thanks." Abigail walked over to her, feeling hesitant if she would talk to her or not. "Hey, Lydia. How's it going?"

Lydia was surprised to see Abigail, but not in the sense of wanting to chat with her. She replied with a simple "hey" then walked away and continued to work.

Abigail followed her. "Lydia, can I talk to you for a minute, please?"

"I didn't make it. Is that what you wanna hear?" Her voice was firm yet soft, not wanting to make a scene.

"Please hear me out, Lydia, I was just trying to—"

"I don't wanna hear it. You haven't supported me up to this point, and you probably never will." Lydia walked away, shaking her head.

"I'm sorry you're not going on to nationals, but even more so about what you're going through." Abigail followed her around the store. "I'm here for you, I always have been. So please, let me carry your burdens."

"I can carry my own, ok?" Lydia took a deep breath. "Besides, how can you help me carry my burdens when you're one of them?"

Abigail knew she had to be patient, which is why she prepared herself to tackle every striking word that would possibly come out of Lydia's irreverent mouth.

"Sorry you feel this way. But even if you would have made it, your happiness wouldn't have lasted forever. Putting faith in material success never does." Abigail knew her comment wouldn't please her, but she continued to express her heart. "There are so many people who have fame and success, but they lack a peace of mind because they don't have the Lord in their lives."

Abigail was surprised how she was given the chance to be heard. She wondered if Lydia finally understood what she was trying to tell her.

"Please, Lydia, do not let your heart be troubled. Let the Lord handle this, let Him give you His peace and comfort—the peace and comfort which the world cannot give. I'm not saying this to overwhelm you, or to upset you."

"Some preacher you are. You've done nothing but upset me, trying to mess up my dream. I bet you're happy now since you got what you wanted, right? Looks like all your prayers for me have been answered. You probably jumped for joy in your heart as soon as I told you I'm not going to nationals. You know what, I'm done with you."

"I didn't jump for joy, Lydia, but I am relieved." With her head hung low, she wiped the tears from her eyes as she followed Lydia around the store again.

"I told you before...I'm trying to help my family, ok?"

"I know, but—"

"Can I please do my job now?" Lydia's loud remark made everyone turn their heads.

"Sorry." Abigail's apology was more directed to the customers than to Lydia.

Lydia walked away, hoping Abigail wouldn't follow her this time. Abigail stood still for a minute, contemplating Lydia's nonverbal hint. If she stayed, she could make things worse, so she decided to leave.

Abigail walked a short distance from Lydia's work and sat down on a public bench. She lifted her head up and prayed. "Dear Lord, I don't know what else to do. Lydia's having such a hard time, but so am I. It's obvious I'm not getting through to her, so I'm releasing everything into Your hands. Please open the eyes of her heart to see You whether or not it's through me. And Lord, please restore our friendship." Seconds later, the bus arrived. It was time for Abigail to head home.

Lydia's stressful day had come to an end. She crossed the road and walked to the bus stop, ready to go home. But since no one was there, it made her wonder if she had missed the bus. As she waited for the next bus to arrive, she checked her phone, but then she looked up when she heard footsteps. It was a homeless man who had asked her if she had a quarter to spare. She reached into her purse and gave him a dollar instead. This made the man very happy. He thanked Lydia and then went his way.

His departure didn't last long—for he had returned within seconds.

"Excuse me, sister. I felt the need to give this to you." He handed her a small pamphlet. Lydia looked at him, wondering why the man in need wanted to give her something in return. But she didn't want to turn him down, so she thanked him. He smiled and turned back around, but this time she watched him leave. As he crossed the lawn, he never looked back.

Lydia looked at the pamphlet, but never opened it. Her gaze, however, was fixed on the cover. The title *The Sacrificed Lamb* was written above a picture of a lamb in bold letters. She looked into the eyes of the lamb and smiled. It was as if the lamb was speaking to her, giving her some sort of comfort.

Without hesitation, Lydia spoke back. "You look so cute. Why would somebody sacrifice you?" She felt compassion toward the lamb, but she did not understand why. Bringing her gaze up, she spotted the homeless man again. He crossed the road and went inside the grocery store—the one next to her work place.

A short time later, Lydia saw him coming out of the store with a small brown paper bag. He walked up to a man who was sitting on the ground, not too far from the store. This struck Lydia as odd. When she left work, no one was sitting near the grocery store. In fact, no one was there the entire time she had been waiting at the bus stop.

She watched the homeless man crouch down, taking a seat next to the other man, who looked to be homeless himself. He opened the bag and handed the man some food. Lydia was amazed to see such kindness. For she had only seen such wonderful deeds on the media, but never in person. Then all of a sudden, it had hit her! The dollar she gave the homeless man wasn't only for him. He had used it to buy food, so he could share it with his friend. But she felt so bad because she knew a dollar wasn't enough to feed them both.

Lydia wanted to buy more food for the men, but she didn't want to risk missing the next bus after such a long wait. If more people had commuted on her route, then the waiting period would be longer, which would then allow her to help the men in need. It was so hard for her to sit back, doing nothing to repay the man for his kindness. So she got up and walked to the store, hoping to return as quickly as possible before the bus arrived.

The long line scared Lydia off, but she was determined not to leave the store without getting more food. She got in line and kept an eye on the bus stop through the window. Finally, it was her turn to cash out. With a brown paper bag of her own, she walked out of the store, but to her dismay—the bus had arrived. She didn't know what to do: run to catch the bus before it left, or stick with her original plan.

Lydia made a beeline toward the men, but it was too late. The bus drove away. She was a bit disappointed, but she also knew she would catch the next ride home. With several minutes to spare, a smile slid across her face, knowing what was more important. She slowed her pace and approached the men.

"Hi. This is for the both of you." Lydia handed them each a sandwich, wrapped in foil.

"Thank you so much!" said the men in unison. Their faces lit up when they unwrapped their sandwiches.

"Aren't you the young girl who was sitting across the street, waiting for the bus?" asked the homeless man who gave her the pamphlet.

"Yes, I am," replied Lydia.

The man looked to his friend. "She gave me a dollar, and I got us something to eat." He shifted his gaze back to Lydia. "Thanks a lot, baby doll."

"Yeah, thanks a lot." The other man smiled at Lydia.

"No problem. I just didn't think the dollar was enough to feed you guys." She smiled at the first homeless man. "I saw what you did for your friend, which was super awesome of you."

"That's what we gotta do, baby doll. He's my friend and he was hungry. I had to share with him, you know?"

Lydia smiled as she nodded. "The kindness you displayed is rare. Something I never saw until today. You inspired me to do the same."

"Means a lot. Thanks," said the homeless man.

The other man spoke up. "Daniel is the only friend I have...he's rescued me so many times."

"Wow. You're like a hero." Lydia beamed at Daniel—the man who asked for a quarter to feed his friend.

Daniel's face lit up at her compliment. "Now that you know my name, what's yours?"

"Lydia."

"Lydia?"

"Yep, Lydia."

"That's a beautiful name," replied Daniel.

A light shade of pink flushed her cheeks. "Thanks."

"So tell me, Lydia, do you have a good friend?" asked Daniel.

Lydia was taken aback by his blunt and unexpected question. She wrestled with what to say, trying to figure out if she still considered Abigail her best friend or not.

"You know, like a friend you can count on." Daniel could tell she was struggling with his question.

"Uh...yeah. I do," replied Lydia halfheartedly.

"For me, that's him right there." Daniel pointed at Joshua. "It's good to have a friend you can trust and count on. A friend who'll try to protect you from bad people and situations. I'm telling you, there's a lot of bad stuff out in the world. If it wasn't for Joshua, I wouldn't be here today. But I'm not the only one he looks after, you know? He's a man chosen by God to lead us to the promised land along with helping us *not* to lose hope while we're still on this earth."

Daniel seemed as if he were giving his life testimony in front of a small congregation, a congregation of one—Lydia. He spoke with such passion, wanting Lydia to truly understand the significance of how God helped him through his friend Joshua.

CHAPTER 3

When Daniel talked, it sounded incomprehensible at times, but Lydia listened as if he was narrating her life story, including her friendship with Abigail.

"You see, Lydia, I'm living life because of a second chance. Thanks to a merciful God," began Daniel. "I had lung cancer two years ago, and my chance of living on this earth was limited. Actually there was no hope. I saw a doctor almost every month due to all the complications. But since Joshua is a man of faith, he prayed to the Lord without ceasing, day and night, until I received my healing."

When Lydia heard the word *cancer*, she was drawn to Daniel even more. But she wasn't sure about the rest of his testimony—the part when he told her about his healing.

"Can you explain how it happened? How you became cancer-free." Lydia was eager for more answers.

"I'm telling you, Lydia. One minute I was sick, then the next I was healed. I know it sounds silly, and hard to believe, but I was healed instantly. God used this man"— he looked over at Joshua—"to take away my infirmity that affected me for so many years. When people who knew me saw and heard what had happened, they were stunned, just like you are now. The thing is, when people look at Joshua, they ignore him and pass him by. They don't want anything to do with a homeless person. But, the Lord has put something mighty inside of him— Joshua has a gift to end people's pain. And because of this, I'm so thankful to the Lord for Joshua. He used my friend to end my physical and spiritual sickness."

"Well, as I said before, I just do what I'm supposed to. All the glory and honor go to Him. I might be the one who is asking for help tomorrow, you know what I'm saying?" Joshua's humility was sincere, and it was evident that Lydia was humbled by it. "If we don't pray for one another, or look after each other, we can't survive this life. You said your name is Lydia, right?"

Lydia nodded. "Yeah."

"Did you get a chance to look at the pamphlet I gave you?" asked Daniel.

"I just looked at the cover," replied Lydia.

"You should make the time to check it out," said Joshua. "It has stories about God's mercy, righteousness, love, and forgiveness...along with His ultimate gift of salvation that He provided to humanity."

Lydia knew the bus would be arriving any minute, but she continued to pay close attention to all Joshua had to say. She crossed her arms over her stomach, feeling encouraged by Joshua's and Daniel's testimonies.

"Thanks for making the time to listen to what we had to say." Joshua smiled at Lydia.

"Not a problem," Lydia replied. "I'm actually learning a lot from you guys."

"Lydia, if you take some time with Joshua, you'll learn a lot more," said Daniel. He was done talking for the moment, so he finished eating sandwich, and then made himself comfortable on the uneven ground.

Lydia was deeply touched by Daniel's peculiar report. She wanted to know more about his sickness and the healing he received.

"How did you get lung cancer?" asked Lydia.

Daniel summed up his past in a short amount of time, knowing Lydia would be leaving very soon. "...I received my healing years ago."

Joshua added to Daniel's testimony. "That's right. This man had cancer, but the healing hands of the Lord touched him. He's been free of cancer for about two or three years now. Right, Daniel?"

"It's been two years," confirmed Daniel.

"Wow! Two years of a cancer-free life," stated Lydia more to herself than to the men.

"That's right." Daniel was grateful to see the Lord working in Lydia. Her glowing countenance was proof of that. "If it wasn't for you and Joshua, I might have starved today. But there was times when I almost did. Either way, I'm able to enjoy every day because of the rest and peace I have in my life. Which is the most important thing I learned from Joshua...the man who introduced me to my Savior. Eternal salvation is the ultimate gift you can receive from God—the source of all gifts."

Joshua and Daniel could see traces of uncertainty etched across Lydia's face concerning their accounts.

"Hey, Lydia, do you believe God can do miracles in someone's life?" asked Joshua. He wanted to challenge her look of ambiguity.

"I'm not sure." Lydia was bounded by her own subject matter that awaited her at home.

Joshua was stunned to hear someone say that the Almighty God, in His absolute understanding, could not perform miracles. He has seen many miracles in his life and in the lives of others.

"He is most certainly the God of miracles." Joshua spiritually prepared himself to plead his case, proving to anyone who disputed God's omnipotence, which included Lydia. "Let me tell you something, Lydia, you can be assured that I'm a true witness to Daniel's supernatural healing."

He didn't wait for Lydia to respond, or to agree with him. Instead, he continued to share the Lord's goodness with her.

"When I was twelve years old, I was sick, and my family wasn't sure what was going on with me. I couldn't walk or talk," Joshua started. "My family tried everything they could to save my life because the doctors couldn't do anything. So, they took me to a church and the whole congregation prayed for me. The Lord spoke through them, telling me I would walk again and be a witness before everybody. A few weeks later, I started to get better, and then one day, I was completely healed. Years had past before I went back to that church, and when I was there, I stood before the congregation and testified."

Joshua gave Lydia some time to digest all he had spoken.

He took a deep breath and continued, "When I was eighteen, I was hit by a car and left to die. It happened at night and there was no one to witness. But thank God I wasn't hurt too bad. I got up like nothing had happened and then went my way home, praising the Lord. Again, not too long ago, like six months before, I found my best friend Jacob. I used to tell him a lot about Jesus, but he never listened. He really didn't care about the Lord or the Bible. Unlike Jacob, I was born and raised in a Christian family...Anyways, since we lived close to each other, we went to the same high school, and became the best of friends. Even though I worried about being friends with someone whose belief and perception countered mine, the Lord had put compassion inside my heart so I could pray for him, leading him to the right path in life. But toward the end of the school year, he was all about gambling and partying. Our friendship started to wither because Jacob didn't want to listen to anything I had to say about the Lord. One of the reasons why he became so angry was because his father got sick. He loved his father very much, so he questioned God, asking why He allowed his father to get sick, letting him suffer."

Joshua's last statement gave Lydia the chills. She wondered if there was an absolute answer to the question she just heard since she had the exact same question about her mother.

"...and I asked him, 'Jacob, why would you be mad at God who you don't even know?' You wanna know his answer? Because he mostly heard about the Lord from me, instead of from personal experience. He didn't understand who God truly was. So I asked Jacob how he could ask such a question, expecting God's interception in his father's life when he didn't care to know Him. Jacob became more involved with drugs and alcohol, going against God and His will because of the influences his peers from school had on him. Despite Jacob's anger and rebellion, I cried out to the Lord for the healing of his father, and for the transformation of his own life. But he wasn't the only one with problems—I was dealing with family issues of my own. My dad was living on the edge and became bedridden for a long time due to an accident at work. Unfortunately, he didn't make it. I was so heartbroken, but I was able to move forward by the comfort and grace of God."

The bus could have arrived, but Lydia would not have noticed. She was too invested in hearing about Joshua's trials and tribulations, including his best friend Jacob's.

Joshua continued, "I couldn't hold on to my job because I had to be with my dad till the last minute. I got fired and evicted from my house, so here I am—today. But, I still believe there's hope. I've been looking for a job and I believe God will provide one. Anyways, back to my friend's story. I found Jacob six months ago and he told me about his dad's healing, and that he had returned to work. I was very happy for him, even more so since he was, and still is, my best friend. Know what I mean? He also told me he got saved, becoming a born-again Christian. That's all what matters to me, which is why I always told him about the Lord, wanting him to live in freedom and liberty as the Bible tells us, 'It is for freedom that Christ has set us free. Stand firm, then, and do not let yourselves be burdened again by a yoke of slavery.' Now he's a fellow brother-in-Christ and our friendship has been renewed. He felt guilty for not caring about my situation, and in turn, he didn't think he deserved God's favor. But I told him we are all saved, not because of the righteous things we had done, or do, but because of His mercy...."

Lydia's brows bunched together. It was difficult for her to digest, and to understand, everything Joshua had said. The more he continued to share his story, the more she was able to relate. It seemed as if he was narrating her life, including her friendship with Abigail.

"Maybe you don't view it as a miracle, but it is." Joshua locked his gaze into Lydia's. "Actually, it was the greatest of all miracles because I was able to see the fruit of my labor, which was to redeem my best friend and his family. I've seen miracles, one after another. I know my dad is in a better place, and I believe I'll see him one day. But maybe you're still wondering why I'm going through all of this: being homeless and jobless, that is. I don't know why certain things happen, but all I can say is that the LORD is righteous in all His ways. All things work together for good to those who love God, to those who are called according to His purpose. I can't ask for anything more than a second chance in life. He has made me the salt to those who have lost the flavor of life while being a light to those who are walking in darkness. And because of that, I am blessed."

"Wow! You've never told me this, Joshua," exclaimed Daniel. "You just gave me a leap of faith."

Due to the nature of the story that looked coincidental, Lydia wasn't sure how to respond, or how to end her conversation with Joshua and Daniel.

In a quick but polite way, Lydia said, "Thanks for sharing your stories."

"I hope you got something important from our testimonies, Lydia. And remember, there is *nothing* impossible with God."

Lydia didn't say anything, which indicated to Joshua that she was still not swayed by his, or Daniel's, conversation with her.

A few seconds later, Lydia added, "It's really hard for me to put together what you both shared with me."

"I understand, Lydia. We're not surprised how hard it is for you to accept what we just told you, and believe me, we did not tell you our stories to convince you about the Lord. Or to make you become like us—a couple of crazy guys about our God. We just told you what we have seen and have gone through in our lives, hoping you can see His loving and kind nature," replied Joshua. "And one more thing, He's able to answer whatever questions you might have about life."

"Well, I guess I have the same question as your friend—why?"said Lydia.

Joshua had a feeling that Lydia correlated the story of his friend Jacob to perhaps her own.

"Lydia, I can't answer you in the same way I did to my friend Jacob because we just met. I don't know anything about you or your way of life. But the Lord does."

"Hey Joshua, do you still have an extra pamphlet, the one filled with heavenly stories?" asked Daniel.

Joshua was not sure what Daniel was talking about.

"The one you read to me when you told me about the Lord for the first time," clarified Daniel. "You know, the story about the lamb."

"Oh, that pamphlet." Joshua's eyes lit up. "Speaking of, I think you should give one to Lydia. It may help to answer her question."

"I already gave her one," responded Daniel.

"Yeah. It's right here." Lydia reached into her jeans pocket and pulled out a handful of crumpled up paper, which included the pamphlet. She was embarrassed for treating it like an unimportant piece of paper. "I'm sorry, I didn't have anywhere else to put it."

"It's ok," replied Joshua. The last thing he wanted was for Lydia to feel bad.

"You gotta read it, Lydia. Or Joshua can read it to you. It's a wonderful story. A story that changed my life." Daniel beamed.

"It's ok, I'll read it myself," replied Lydia, "while I wait for the bus."

Joshua and Daniel were not sure what to make of her response. They didn't know if she had a lack of interest to know more about God, or if she was in a hurry to get back home.

"As I told you before, it talks all about God's character and His response to humanity." Joshua felt a heaviness for Lydia. "You'll find answers about the meaning of life too."

"It's true, Lydia. It gives you the answers that you might be wondering about your life," added Daniel.

"But what if my questions are too hard to answer? What if they can't be answered at all?" Lydia believed God worked in the lives of others—how He worked in Joshua's and Daniel's lives, but when it came to her, she doubted He would do the same.

"Believe me...there is no question too hard to be answered as long as you bring it to Him. There are many ways He answers our prayers, Lydia. And a lot of times, He works through others to help those in need. So my question is, are you willing to share your story?" Joshua silently prayed for God to open up Lydia's heart, giving her the courage, strength and peace she needed to do so.

Lydia tensed up and wrung her hands together. It was evident to Joshua and Daniel that she was reluctant to share her story.

"It's ok, Lydia. Whenever you feel up to it, talk to God about what's in your heart, and I guarantee you, He will answer," said Joshua.

"I think sometimes we're meant to live with unanswered questions, you know?" Lydia recklessly debunked Joshua's promise about God's response to prayers.

Joshua and Daniel were consumed by silence, not knowing how to respond to Lydia's out-of-the-blue remark.

"Life is like a puzzle, and trying to find the pieces that fit, can be super hard. And sometimes, you can't find the pieces at all." Lydia's voice intensified with resistance. "It's really hard for me to process anything spiritual. But I'm not saying you guys are wrong. I truly respect your beliefs, and for sharing your stories. To be honest, though, I don't believe in those type of stories. I mean, it might be true for you"—Lydia turned to face Daniel—

"about not having cancer anymore. But it's possible to be cancer-free if someone follows their doctor's orders along with finishing up their treatment."

"Lydia, I was at the final stage, and the doctor told me I had months to live," replied Daniel. Tears of joy filled his eyes as he thought about the miracle he had received, but at the same time, they were tears of sorrow due to Lydia's unbelief. "But God said I shall not die, but live, and declare the works of the Lord. Just like I'm doing now—to you. I don't care if you believe me or not, but you're hearing a living testimony."

"I don't know if your question is greater, or equal to Daniel's, Lydia. But I still encourage you to come to the Lord with all your doubts, fears, questions, and hardships," said Joshua.

"Well, I probably do have the exact same question," stated Lydia matter-of-factly.

Joshua was not sure what she was trying to say. "I may not be able to solve your toughest problems, but I can present them before the Almighty One."

Lydia was feeling more uncomfortable than before. She turned and walked away, not wanting to get her hopes up with a belief she claimed, and yet refused, to believe in. Her attention, however, still lingered on their testimonies. Healing for her mother, and restoration for her friendship with Abigail, is what she needed. Still, she kept on walking.

"As Daniel said before, we may look miserable on this earth, but we have internal peace, which surpasses all understanding," said Joshua.

Lydia refrained from taking another step—Joshua had caught her attention.

"I don't know what kind of life challenges or questions you have, but when you gave me what you had, what I needed, I didn't think it was fair to walk away without giving you what I had," concluded Daniel.

"And I appreciate that." Lydia placed the pamphlet back into the pocket of her jeans, and then she looked at her phone to check the time. "I gotta go. Nice talking to the both of you."

"Take care." Daniel smiled as she walked away.

"It was great talking to you, Lydia," added Joshua. "By any chance, do you have a Bible?" Joshua shouted that time. He knew the question was awkward, knowing where she stood in her faith, or lack thereof. But either way, he had to know.

"Yeah. I think I do!" shouted Lydia. Even if she *didn't* have one, she would have told them that she did. She was ready to put their questions at rest, not wanting to talk about God, the Bible, and her problems any longer.

"Are you sure!" asked Joshua.

"Yep!" replied Lydia. She kept walking but then she came to a halt. Turning around, she headed back toward Joshua and Daniel. She had to ask just one more question, a question she would regret if she didn't. "Could you keep my mom in your prayers?"

Joshua did not expect Lydia to return, let alone to return with a prayer request. "Of course we will, Lydia. But is your mom ok?"

Pressing her lips together, Lydia shook her head *no*.

"God is the God of love, and He never rules anybody by force, but by choice. Lydia, I suggest you choose His loving call and mercy. I know you're a kind-hearted person because of your action toward me," said Daniel. "And if you make the Lord the center of your life, you will never lack anything good. He will always make a way for you—even when it seems there isn't one."

"Thanks." Lydia turned around and headed back to the bus stop.

"Make sure to read the pamphlet!" shouted Daniel.

"We will pray for you and your mom, Lydia. But don't forget to read your Bible. Read John 3:16!" Joshua's voice followed Lydia like a gentle, warm breeze.

Lydia didn't turn around, but nodded her head in response to Joshua's last comment. She made it to the bus stop just in time. Gazing out the window, she waved to Joshua and Daniel as she headed home.

CHAPTER 4

Out of curiosity, Lydia decided to take Daniel's advice. She fished inside her jeans pocket and pulled out the pamphlet—it was filled with parables from the Bible. She flipped through the pages and came across a timely message that her soul desperately needed.

The Sacrificed Lamb

Behold, the Sacrificed Lamb stands at the door, and knocks: if any man hear His voice, and open the door, He will come in...

Lydia read nonstop until she reached her destination. She got off the bus and walked home, unable to get the Lamb's story out of her mind. The quote Joshua shouted at her as she walked to the bus stop echoed in her thoughts as well—John 3:16. Feeling deeply convicted, Lydia was willing to give the Lord a chance.

When Lydia arrived at her house, she headed straight for the bookshelf located in the living room. After staring at the forgotten book covered in dust, she reached for it and then wiped it off with her hand. An elegant font, inscribed in gold, revealed the title *Holy Bible*.

Lydia had been reading the Bible for some time, but there was a particular verse that charmed her:

"Is anyone among you sick? Let them call the elders of the church to pray over them and anoint them with oil in the name of the Lord. And the prayer offered in faith will make the sick person well; the Lord will raise them up. If they have sinned, they will be forgiven."

Lydia didn't want to disclose her life transformation to anyone, especially to her best friend, Abigail. She feared it would be a sign of defeat, validating Abigail's rejection of her dream to win the singing contest. Despite that, she started to realize why her best friend was admired among her classmates and teachers.

A few weeks following her self-scheduled time to read the Bible, Lydia had developed some faith in the Word of God. She also came to a point in wanting to attend a church, in hopes of finding someone to pray for her mother.

Lydia took the same route to get to school and work, but she had never noticed the local church located in her neighborhood until today. Since it was her day off, Lydia stopped by the church and picked up the weekly program. She spent time reading it throughout the week, wanting to get somewhat familiar with the church before going back.

After some time, she felt more confident, so she paid the church another visit. She walked up to the church sign and stared at the pastor's name. Then, she walked into the main entrance of the church and encountered a woman sitting at the front desk—the church secretary.

"Good morning. How can I help you, my dear?" The woman's voice was soft, her smile inviting.

"Hi, uh...can I talk to Pastor Paul?" asked Lydia. She was grateful to have memorized his name from the sign out front.

"I think Pastor Paul is about to leave. Is he expecting you?"

"Uh...no. I just want to see him."

She looked at Lydia, not knowing what else to say. For she had wondered why this young girl needed to see him.

"Ok, honey." The woman stood to her feet and extended her hand toward Lydia, welcoming her with another smile. "My name is Grace and it's nice to meet you."

She returned the smile. "Same. And my name's Lydia."

"Please have a seat, and I'll check to see if Pastor Paul is still in his office." Grace paused and looked at the bag sitting on her desk. "Actually, he should be here because this is his bag. Give me a minute, I'll be right back."

"Ok, thanks." Lydia sat down and looked around the lobby. She anticipated Grace's return, hoping the pastor would be with her.

A short while later, a decent-looking man with gray hair walked through the front entrance of the church. He then entered the lobby, looking a little frazzled, as if he had forgotten something. But then he noticed Lydia as he walked toward the lobby.

"Hi there, young lady." He reached for the bag sitting on the desk. "Is someone helping you?"

Lydia was suspicious, thinking he could be the man that she was looking for, especially since he took the bag that Grace said belonged to Pastor Paul.

"Yeah," replied Lydia. "I need to talk to the pastor, so the secretary went to check if he's still here." Her nerves were getting the best of her, thinking Grace would never return.

"So you want to see Pastor Paul?" He looked into Lydia's eyes with a puzzled look—she had no clue she was talking to the man she wanted to see.

"Yeah," said Lydia once again. She wondered why Grace was taking so long to return.

"Well, guess what? Here he is, standing before you." His humorous but kind introduction took Lydia by surprise. "I'm Pastor Paul, and how lucky you are to meet him, ha!"

"Oh, wow!" Lydia jumped up from her seat. "I'm Lydia, nice to meet you."

"Great to meet you, too, Lydia. How may I help you?"

Their conversation was interrupted by Grace's clomping footsteps coming from the other side of the room.

"I'm afraid he is not"—Grace looked up and smiled—"there you are, Pastor Paul! This beautiful young lady was looking for you."

"Yes, we were just getting to know each other," replied Pastor Paul.

"Well, that's wonderful. At first, I thought you would be in your office, but when I didn't see you, I checked the prayer room," said Grace.

The pastor chuckled. "I *was* in my office but then I left. And as I walked away from the church, I realized I had forgotten my bag. So I came back to retrieve it."

Pastor Paul switched his gaze over to Lydia and picked up the conversation where they had left off.

"Are you a member of our church, Lydia?" He couldn't recall if they had met before.

"Uh, no. I'm not." Lydia worried, wondering if membership was required to request a prayer.

"No problem, my dear. But do you attend church somewhere else?" This question was worse than the first one.

"I, I used to go to church with my mom, when I was a kid." Lydia hoped her response would keep the next possible question at bay: *Are you even a Christian?*

"I see. Have a seat, my dear," said Pastor Paul.

Lydia sat in the same seat as before, feeling hopeful yet anxious.

He turned back to Grace. "Would you please let Nathan know I'm coming? He's in my car, in the front parking lot."

"Oh, Nathan's here? You should have sent him in to get your bag," replied Grace.

"I would have, but he's on the phone with his good friend Caleb. I didn't want to interrupt him."

Grace nodded. "Understandable."

"Thanks for letting him know, Grace." Pastor Paul turned back to Lydia and smiled. "Forgetting my bag may have been planned by the Lord. Perhaps you and I meeting is the perfect will of the Lord. Don't you think?"

Lydia squirmed in her chair. "Maybe." She was not sure if this was coincidental or divinely orchestrated.

"As for me, I agree with Pastor Paul." Grace beamed and then made her way toward the front door, her heels clomping behind her.

"Well, shall we step out in faith to find out?" He grabbed a chair and placed it across from Lydia, wanting to speak with her face to face.

"Sure."

Lydia was a tad bit apprehensive, but she was eager to share her heart with someone she felt she could trust.

"So, uh. I started reading the Bible a few weeks ago, and I came across a Scripture where it talks about asking someone from the church to pray for a person who's sick. Well, my mom's very sick, so can you please come and pray for her?"

"What's wrong with her, my dear?" Pastor Paul knitted his brows.

"She has pancreatic cancer," began Lydia. "And she has no choice but to stay home, waiting for her cure. But I don't know if that will ever happen." Lydia's hopelessness was heavy, and Pastor Paul could sense it.

"I'm really sorry to hear that, Lydia. But there is hope. And by you seeking God's Word along with coming here—are the two most important steps you have taken to head in the right direction."

A gentle smile slid across Lydia's face. "Thanks. That makes me feel a lot better."

"You're welcome." He smiled and continued, "Now, about the Bible talking about calling on the elders of the church to pray over the sick in the name of the Lord, you're right about that too. With that said, is your mother getting any treatment?"

"Yeah she is, but she's so tired of being on and off of her treatment. We can't help it, though. Without insurance, it's hard to pay for the medications, treatments, and doctor's bills to keep her healthy. It's been a while since my mom stopped working, so I'm trying to support her with my summer job." Lydia's eyes overflowed with tears. "It helps to pay for some of her medications, but it's not enough."

She hoped her request for prayer didn't come off as an appeal for assistance.

"You are phenomenal, Lydia. I really appreciate you coming here and sharing your story." Compassion illuminated Pastor Paul's eyes. "I will definitely pray for your mother. And for you. I believe the Lord will heal her, so continue to have faith, ok? We'll also help your mother in whatever ways we're able to."

Lydia nodded, feeling reassured. His willingness to talk with her, including his genuineness, made her feel like she could tell him everything that was on her mind.

"I love my mom so much...she raised me by herself and I owe her big time. I've tried everything I could to help her, but I'm running out of resources. I even participated in a singing contest that we had at our school, thinking it would help to get my mom the treatment she needs." Lydia was afraid to reveal her other goal of entering the contest, worrying Pastor Paul would think her selfish. With a soft voice, she continued, "It was also a chance to pursue my dream, but it didn't happen."

"What was your dream, Lydia?"

"To become a star. But only because I thought it would help, and change my family's life for good." A nervous, sarcastic laugh exposed her regret and disappointment.

Pastor Paul scooted his chair closer and then rested his hand on Lydia's shoulder. "I'm really sorry about your mother, but you're doing everything you can to help her. And the Lord knows this. To you, it may seem like your options to help are running out, but I believe the Lord is just getting started with you and your mother. He wants to take control of your circumstances, but in order to do so, you need to allow Him."

Pastor Paul looked at Lydia to see if she was ready to surrender to God.

Due to the fear of giving up control, Lydia's eyes welled up with tears once again, her heart thumping desperately. But yet at the same time, the hope of not having to endure this journey alone, soothed her uncertainties. With that, she nodded her head in agreement.

CHAPTER 5

Lydia, you are not here by coincidence. You are here just at the right time, at the right place. Maybe the path you were going, was not the will of God. But be encouraged because He is above all our circumstances." Pastor Paul leaned forward to give her shoulder a gentle squeeze, and then scooted back in his chair. "The Lord has greater and better plans for you. So please don't regret what didn't happen, ok? Most importantly, don't assume the success you can achieve in this world will solve all your problems, or to fulfill the lack within."

Pastors Paul's words resonated with Lydia, reminding her of the conversations she had with her best friend. Abigail had cautioned her about the world's ways, and how striving for fame was a dangerous path to venture on. And that she wouldn't find peace through her own venue.

A tear slid down Lydia's face. "My friend used to tell me the same thing."

"Maybe this is a confirmation from the Holy Ghost, letting you know what you've heard is true. Would you be here today if all your dreams were fulfilled, including all the success you could have in this world?"

"I don't know." Lydia shrugged. "I guess not."

"Lydia, your dreams of success by winning the singing contest would have given your mother a little extra time on this earth, but it wouldn't have saved her. The Lord is the only One who is able to give her the breath of life here and now—and in the life to come. Everything works for good, for those who are called according to the will of God, as the Bible says."

He gave Lydia some time to process all he had said before asking her his next question.

"I am so grateful you've started reading your Bible, but have you accepted Jesus into your life as your personal Savior?"

"Uh..." Lydia wasn't sure what he meant.

"Are you a born-again Christian?"

Her eyes lit up with understanding. "Yeah, I'm a Christian."

"If you don't mind, will you please allow me to clarify myself?"

Lydia nodded her approval.

"Being a Christian compared to being a born-again Christian, is totally different. There are people who refer to themselves as Christians, using it more as a title. But when someone is truly born again, it means that person has been spiritually reborn from God, becoming part of the body of Christ. This how one can develop a personal relationship with the Lord. I'll be very honest, the cost of doing so may be great, but down the road, it will all be worth it."

Lydia became perplexed again, not understanding Pastor Paul's calculation of salvation's cost and rewards.

"I don't know if you got to the point in your Bible which says, 'Peace I leave with you, My peace I give to you; not as the world gives do I give to you. Let not your heart be troubled, neither let it be afraid.' That was Jesus talking to His disciples." He paused, giving Lydia time to receive this truth as well. "It is very important for you to know the Lord as your personal Savior before anything else. You know why?"

Lydia shrugged again. Not because she was clueless, but because of worrying her answer would not be the correct one.

"Because it gives you strength to pray for your mother, yourself, and for others."

I thought you were gonna pray for my mom, not me, thought Lydia.

"That's actually why I stopped by...to ask if you could come and pray for my mom."

"Ok, my dear, not a problem. I just wanted to remind you that your salvation comes first, and I can pray for you right now, if you're willing to accept Jesus as your personal Savior."

Lydia remained silent. It seemed to her that Pastor Paul was insinuating that he wouldn't go to her mother and pray for her, unless she accepted Jesus. He discerned this right away, so he asked the Holy Ghost in silence to help him out.

"I really don't mind to come and pray for your mother, but the healing of our spiritual sickness should come first, so we can become whole to the will of the Lord. Anybody who does not have Jesus in his or her life, lacks something very important, which is eternal salvation. When one is truly saved, they are free from sin and its consequences, but when one is not, they will be separated from the living God for eternity. The Bible says, 'Behold, now is the favorable time; behold, now is the day of salvation.' So Lydia, you must decide. I can feel and see how God is orchestrating everything in your life, which is why you and I are having this conversation."

Minutes filled the silence between them as Lydia pondered everything they had talked about. Her conversations, more like disputes, she had with Abigail surfaced to her conscious as well. She couldn't deny the fact of how hard and scary it was to help her mother on her own. But more than anything, she needed a personal relationship with the Lord—the only One who could truly guide and help her in this life. The only One who could give her eternal life. Lydia finally agreed to accept Jesus as her personal Savior. Pastor Paul took her hand and then they bowed their heads.

"Dear heavenly Father, I thank you for giving me this opportunity. I know I'm a sinner and I ask you to forgive my sins. I believe that Jesus died on the cross for my sins and rose from the dead. I accept Jesus Christ as my Lord and personal Savior. Come into my heart and be the Lord of my life. Thank you for your forgiveness and mercy. In Jesus's name. Amen."

Pastor Paul congratulated Lydia for inviting Jesus into her life and told her to keep reading her Bible. He also told her about the importance of discipleship now that she was a born- again Christian. Following Pastor Paul's prayer and mini sermon, Lydia thanked him along with reminding him why she stopped by the church in the first place.

"So, will you still come and pray for my mom?"

"Of course, my dear. Where do you live?"

"Nearby," replied Lydia. "Like walking distance from here."

The familiar sound of clomping heels signified Grace's return. "Pastor Paul, Nathan wants to know how much longer you'll be."

"Thanks, Grace, I'm on my way." He looked at Lydia with apologetic eyes. "Do you mind staying here with Grace while I'll take my son to his game? I'll be back in a few minutes."

"Yeah, that's fine," responded Lydia.

Pastor Paul left the church, rejoicing over Lydia's salvation. But yet there was an urgency that pricked his heart. Lydia's unexpected visitation was a wake-up call. God's children are supposed to go out to reach others rather than the hurting and needy coming to them. Grace had the same conviction, but she was reminded that the One in heaven knows everyone's heart, extending compassion and mercy every day. The Holy Ghost also reminded her that no one is perfect, including those who belong to God.

Grace turned her attention back on Lydia—who was holding a book titled *Today Is Your Day.*

She must have picked it up from the coffee table, thought Grace.

Grace couldn't contain her excitement. "Congratulations, honey, for accepting the Lord as your Savior!"

Lydia looked up and smiled. "Thanks."

"The book you're holding, is a good one. If you'd like, you can borrow it."

"Thanks but maybe next time. I gotta get going." Lydia placed the book back on the table then stood up, fixing the collar of her shirt.

"But don't you want to wait for Pastor Paul? He'll be right back." Worry lines formed on Grace's forehead. She didn't want the pastor's sudden departure to discourage Lydia.

"I do, but I don't wanna keep my mom waiting any longer."

The front door opened and Grace and Lydia turned to see who it was—Pastor Paul had returned quicker than expected.

"Did you forget something, pastor?" asked Grace.

"My obedience," replied Pastor Paul. "I came back to get Lydia." He switched his gaze over to Lydia and smiled. "You ready to go home, so I can pray for her mother?"

Lydia's demeanor became bright and cheerful. "Yes, sir!"

"Grace, would you please drop Nathan off at his football game?"

"Sure, not a problem." Grace smiled. "You came back just in time...Lydia was about to leave."

Contained tears glistened in Pastor Paul's eyes. He was relieved and grateful to return before Lydia had left yet he felt remorse for almost losing his chance to minster and pray for her mother. Grace noticed and teared up as well.

"Sorry but we better leave. It's almost time for my mom to take her medications. And I have to make her something to eat before she does."

Pastor Paul nodded. "No apologies needed, my dear." He said a few words to Grace, grabbed some papers sitting on the desk, and then escorted Lydia out of the church.

The front door closed behind them and Grace prayed on their behalf.

When they got to the car, Lydia asked Pastor Paul if they could walk instead. She told him it was about a five-minute walk, so he agreed.

"Do you know where Shalom is? The grocery store," asked Lydia.

"I sure do." Pastor Paul grinned. "It's my favorite store."

"Mine too. And my house isn't far from it."

As they began walking to Lydia's house, Pastor Paul thought it was a good time to continue their conversation.

"If you don't mind, can you please share how you're feeling?" asked Pastor Paul.

"How I'm feeling?" Lydia's brows bunched together.

He chuckled. "My apologies. What I meant was, how are you feeling about inviting the Lord into your heart?"

"I feel good." Lydia looked straight ahead as she beamed. "Really good."

"That's wonderful to hear, Lydia. And as your relationship with the Lord continues to flourish, so will your joy, peace, and hope." He picked up his pace to match Lydia's. "You remind me of my son, concerning his emotions."

Lydia stopped in her tracks and looked at Pastor Paul with another quizzical look. This made him chuckle again.

"At the end of youth group, they always have a prayer session. And the look of joy and hope on my son's face, including the excitement in his voice, greatly increases my faith. He loves it so much and I have no doubt you will too. If you're interested, come by after our morning service. Or better yet, come to both."

"Oh, ok." Lydia's somber response dampened Pastor's Paul enthusiasm and hope. He was concerned her wariness would hinder the fellowship and discipleship she desperately needed.

"My son is filled with the fire of the Holy Ghost, and I pray he always will be. But my hope is for you to be filled too. I can't help but to marvel when young people exhibit their burning passion for the Lord."

The pastor's comment struck a nerve with Lydia. "Thanks. But I'm not like your son. I'm not a pastor's kid."

"You're right, but when it comes to free will, we all have it."

Pastor Paul's heart ached for Lydia due to her blindness, and lack of knowledge, concerning spiritual matters, including earthly ones.

"Those who are called into ministry, such as pastors as you mentioned, does not mean, or guarantee, the salvation of another. My son made a personal choice to give his life to Christ. All I can do is pray for him, and to lead him in the way he should go."

Time seemed to linger as they walked to Lydia's house, which gave Pastor Paul more time to ponder whether or not to present his next question. But then he remembered she had never mentioned anything about her father. Questions raced through his mind, but the gentle nudge coming from within confirmed what he should say next.

"For being so young and enduring life's hardships, you certainly know how to take it all in stride. There's no doubt about the deep love and respect you have for your mother. But I'm sure there are times when the both of you don't agree on everything, right?"

Lydia's eyes widened. "Uh...right."

"So you see, my son had a chance to follow the right path, or not. Just like you were given a chance. When it comes to repentance, godly living, and eternal salvation, the Lord Himself has never, and *will* never, force His will on anyone."

"Nodding her understanding, Lydia stared ahead, watching her home come into view.

CHAPTER 6

T here it is." Lydia pointed to her house, interrupting
Pastor Paul as he quoted more Scriptures from the
Bible.

She slid the house key into the lock and then opened
the front door. The house was quiet. Lydia called out to
her mother, wondering where she was. She made her way
to the kitchen and Pastor Paul trailed behind. Her mother
wasn't in there. Before worry could set in, Lydia
presumed she was upstairs, taking a nap.

Still, she called for her again. "Mom, are you here?"

"Yes, Lydia, I'm here," came her mother's sluggish
voice.

Pastor Paul remained in the kitchen as Lydia went
upstairs to see her mother.

"Hi, Mom." Lydia walked into the bedroom and saw her mother laying in bed as she had suspected.

"Hi, honey. Where have you been? You never told me you were leaving."

"Sorry, Mom. I was going to, but then I saw you sleeping." Lydia sat on the edge of her bed. "I went to visit someone."

"So who did you go see? Was it Abigail?"

"No. It was someone else."

Ruth raised an emaciated brow. "Was it a new friend?"

"Yeah. You can say that." Lydia reached for her mother's hand and held it gently. "I went to see someone at the local church."

Ruth pulled away from Lydia's grip. "Church?"

"Uh, yeah." Lydia was hurt by her mother's reaction and tone.

"Why did you want to visit someone from a church? It's not even Sunday." Ruth was suspicious that Lydia went to get someone to comfort her. A while back, they had made a policy that Sunday was the only day they would go to church.

A tear escaped the corner of Lydia's eye. "I just wanted to find someone to pray for you. And that person is here, to meet you."

Ruth swallowed the lump of guilt in her throat. She was deeply moved by her daughter's love and concern, but she was also apprehensive to have someone from church in their house.

"Mom, we've been trying so many things to get you better, so I thought prayer could be another option."

"Lydia, for raising you on my own, you've turned out to be such a wonderful daughter. And I'm so grateful. You've always been open to what I had to say along with respecting and obeying me, but you should have told me about seeking help from the church. It makes feel as if this is the last day of my life."

"No, Mom. I was just—"

Ruth interrupted, "The time will come when I may need to be comforted, but I don't need anybody's comfort right now."

"Mom, I'm really sorry. I never thought of it that way."

"It's ok, honey. But I have to decline the offer."

"I understand." Lydia lowered her head, feeling like a failure. "I'll tell Pastor Paul to leave."

Ruth's jaw fell open. "I can't believe you brought the pastor into our house. You know you're supposed to ask me who you can bring over." Ruth pushed the blanket away and gathered her energy to get out of bed. Lydia trailed behind her mother as her stomach twisted in knots. There was no telling what her mother would say to Pastor Paul, and what she would say to her once he left.

Ruth made her entrance into the kitchen. "Hello, sir."

"Hello"—Pastor Paul brought his arm around his back, hiding the Bible in his hand—"you must be Ruth." He smiled but discerned he wasn't welcomed.

"I am," said Ruth matter-of-factly.

"It's a pleasure to meet you." Pastor Paul paused, mentally praying for guidance and peace. "My name's Paul. I'm the senior pastor at the Church of Zion."

"I know." Ruth glared at him. "Lydia said she brought you here to comfort us."

"Yes, but I'm also here to—"

"I'm sorry, but I'm not interested at the moment," interrupted Ruth.

Pastor Paul looked at Lydia, hoping she would intervene.

"Mom," said Lydia sternly. "He just wants to help. Please, just give him a chance."

Ruth turned to face Lydia, silently forbidding her from saying anymore. The anger and harshness from her mother's eyes made Lydia shudder.

"Sir, if the time ever comes for your assistance, I'll let you know," said Ruth.

"Ma'am, I understand. But may I talk to you for a minute about Jesus Christ?"

"Not today, sir." Ruth turned her back on him and then hobbled out of the kitchen. She made her way through the living room and opened the front door. "I need you to leave my house—now."

"I'm sorry to be a bother, ma'am." With sad eyes and slumped shoulders, Pastor Paul made his way out the door. "Have a blessed day."

He glanced over his shoulder and gave Lydia a lopsided grin. He knew she felt as disappointed as he did, and perhaps awkward, due to his presence. The door closed on his face and he let out a heavy sigh.

"Mom, how could you!" Lydia threw arms out in frustration. "He was only trying to help."

Pastor Paul could hear them arguing despite the closed door and windows. He contemplated whether or not to knock on the door, hoping to calm the angry mother and her troubled daughter. But he decided it would be best to walk away, for now.

"Listen to me, Lydia. I expect you to let me know where you are going before you leave the house, ok? And, I would really appreciate it if you would keep quiet about my illness. I don't care if you go to church or not, that's totally up to you. But don't bring anybody to my house unless I approve." She went upstairs and slammed the bedroom door behind her.

Lydia was frozen with shock due to her mother's unusual behavior. Not caring what her mother would think, or say, she flung the front door open. She ran after Pastor Paul, wanting to apologize on her mother's behalf.

"Pastor Paul," shouted Lydia, "wait up!"

He came to a halt and turned around—Lydia was running toward him, out of breath.

"Are you all right, Lydia?"

Lydia stopped to catch her breath. "I'm...I'm really sorry...for what just happened."

"Don't worry, Lydia. In due time, all will be well." Pastor Paul fought against the doubt telling him otherwise.

"I didn't think she would get mad at me. Let alone furious." Hunched over with her hands on her knees,

Lydia drew in deep breaths. "I don't know why she lashed out. It's so embarrassing."

"It's ok." Pastor Paul placed a hand on her shoulder. "Although the situation was tense, I understand why she's so upset. Sometimes, hurting people expect instant relief, answers, or miracles."

"But I didn't ask for any of that," replied Lydia. "I just asked you to pray for her."

"I know."

Pastor Paul wished he could comfort Lydia in an instant himself.

"I have seen a number of people in similar situations. Worry and fear enter their hearts when they're visited from the church to pray for them. It's makes them think as if they're being prepared for their last breath," said Pastor Paul. "But in truth, it's to share with them the reality, knowledge, and hope they can find in God. It's an opportunity to plant seeds of love and truth in those who need it. Deliverance and healing are components of His love."

Pastor Paul signaled to Lydia to move off the street and onto the sidewalk.

"You did the right thing, Lydia, by coming to our church, and asking us to pray for your mother. I want you to be strong in your faith and be persistent in your confidence in the Lord. No matter what."

Lydia nodded, understanding all what Pastor Paul had said. Still, fragments of discouragement snuffed out some of the embers burning within her soul.

"By doing so," Pastor Paul said, "you'll redeem your mother. And I promise, you'll never be alone. The Holy Ghost will always be with you, and so will I."

He reached inside the breast pocket of his suit and took out a notepad.

"Sorry for being old-fashioned, but may I have your number?"

"Sure," replied Lydia, "it's...."

"And if you need anything, give me a call." He ripped out a piece of paper, wrote down his number, and handed it to Lydia. "One more thing before I leave—please don't stop reading your Bible. It's the perfect map for your life, which will guide you through every path with the help of the Holy Ghost."

"Sorry again for asking you to come to my house—all for nothing." Lydia frowned as she stared down at the piece of paper in her hand. But nonetheless, she was somewhat comforted, knowing she could contact him at any time.

"You don't have to be, Lydia. There's nothing to feel bad about." He gave her a gentle pat on the shoulder. "Now go back home and take care of your mother."

"I will. Just hope she's not as angry, though," said Lydia more to herself than to Pastor Paul.

The words from her mother, *My house. My rules,* echoed through her mind.

"Like I said, the Holy Ghost will always be with you. Now go in peace." His genuine smile made Lydia smile too. She sucked in a breath and then turned to leave. As she got closer to her house, she glanced over her shoulder—Pastor Paul was still in view. He waited to make sure she made it home safely.

CHAPTER 7

After a soft rapt to the door, Lydia twisted it open. Her stomach tightened as she entered her mother's room with caution. Ruth was sitting on the edge of the bed, her hand pressed to her head as if she had a terrible headache.

Lydia sat down next to her mother and grabbed her free hand. "I'm sorry, Mom. I didn't mean to upset you."

Ruth looked into Lydia's eyes and gave her a weak smile. "I forgive you, honey. But I'm trying to fight this battle alone, and I don't want anybody to make me feel like I've already failed."

Lydia wanted to reassure her about the true reason for Pastor Paul's visitation, but she decided against her flow of thoughts. "Ok, I understand. Would you like some coffee?"

"Coffee sounds wonderful. Thank you, honey." Ruth closed her eyes and pressed her lips together. The intensity of her headache was obvious to Lydia. "And Lydia, I'm sorry for raising my voice at you."

"It's ok, Mom." Lydia placed a soft kiss on her mother's cheek and then left the room to make a pot of coffee.

The next morning, Lydia grabbed her Bible off the nightstand, and then pressed her back against the headboard. She flipped it open where the silky ribbon marked the last place she had left off the night before.

After reading a few verses, she clasped her hands and prayed. She then went to the kitchen to make breakfast for her mother and herself—she frowned. There was nothing left in the kitchen, except a half bag of cereal and a small amount of milk. She grabbed her purse, but remembered to check with her mother before she left.

She poked her head through the cracked door and saw her mom lying in bed. But she wasn't asleep.

"Morning, Mom."

"Good morning, honey," replied Ruth with a coarse voice.

"I'm gonna go and get something for breakfast."

Ruth slowly propped herself up. "We're all out of food?"

"Pretty much. There's only a small amount of cereal and milk left."

Heat rose to Ruth's face and she turned away. Guilt and shame consumed her for not being able to provide for her daughter.

"Can you hand me my purse, honey?" Ruth pointed to the door knob.

"Sure." Lydia handed the purse to her mother and watched as she rummaged through it.

"I want you to go and get something."

"Don't worry about it, Mom. I have some money."

"You're so sweet, but go get something for yourself to eat. I'm not too hungry, anyway."

Lydia knew her mother was speaking out of guilt. "How about some coffee instead?" She tried to divert her mother's apprehension by offering to make her favorite beverage.

"Sounds good." Ruth forced a smile. "I'll be down in a few."

Ruth stared at the dining room table. The plates and cups were empty. Lydia cleared her throat to get her mother's attention. She pulled out a chair and her mother sat down. A smile slid across Lydia's face as she placed a small paper bag on the table.

"I got us an egg sandwich." Lydia hoped her mother's appetite would return.

"Where did you get this?"

"At the grocery store."

"Let me guess, Shalom?"

Lydia nodded. "I knew I'd have the time to leave before you made it downstairs."

She poured coffee into her mother's cup, filling it halfway. Then she poured the other half in hers and joined her mother at the table.

"Why aren't you having tea?" Ruth knew it was Lydia's favorite drink.

"'Cause I wanna join you today."

Ruth smiled. "Ok. But don't get addicted like me."

Lydia giggled. "Don't worry, I won't. It's just for today."

Both seemed to forget the aftermath of the conflict they had yesterday as they enjoyed their breakfast.

"Did you take your pain medicine?" asked Lydia.

"Yes, earlier today. But it hasn't alleviated the pain. It's killing me." Ruth sighed heavily. "I'll probably have to see Doctor Luke, so he can prescribe something stronger."

"I'm sorry, Mom." Lydia's eyes started to water.

"Don't worry, honey, it'll be all right." Ruth tried her best to put on a brave face, but she and Lydia knew they needed more than help—they needed miracles. "But do promise me you'll save your money for school supplies for next semester. And to help, I have some money you can add to yours." Ruth got up to get her purse.

"Mom, don't worry about it. I'll use mine."

Ruth knew she wouldn't be able to change her daughter's mind, so instead, she shifted their discussion with an unexpected question. "So, when did you start going to church?"

Lydia looked into her mother's. "Actually, yesterday was my first time. I might have mentioned it already, but the church is in our neighborhood."

Ruth scrunched her face, trying to remember if she's seen the church or not.

"The church is next to Shalom," Lydia said. "You know, the grocery store we shop at."

"Right."

"Before I visited the church, I started reading the Bible. There's a Scripture that talks about getting someone from the church to pray for the sick. So it motivated me to seek help. It's weird, though, 'cause I never paid attention to its existence until then. Again, I'm sorry I upset you...I was just trying to help."

"I understand where you're coming from, and it warms my heart how much you love me. Still, I didn't expect someone from the church to pay me a visit. Let alone the head pastor."

"I didn't ask 'cause you would've said no." Lydia crossed her arms over her stomach, fearing their conversation would escalate into another argument.

Ruth felt the tension rising as well. She leaned her chin on her hand and inhaled a much-needed breath. But this didn't stop her from asking more questions. "When did you become a religious person? And where did you get a Bible from?"

"First of all, I don't think I'm a religious person. And as for the Bible, I found it on the bookshelf."

"Really? I had no idea we had one in the house."

"Me either until the time when Abigail challenged me to read it. I searched our bookshelf, and didn't expect to find one, but I did. I stared at it and then changed my mind, so I put it back."

Lydia stood up from her chair and cleared the table. She placed the plates and coffee cups inside the sink.

"So besides that incident with Abigail, what else motivated you to start reading the Bible?"

"It's a long story. Are you sure you wanna know?"

Ruth nodded with enthusiasm. "Yes, please."

"It was a month or so ago—when Abigail and I had an argument."

Concern replaced Ruth's fascination.

"It wasn't anything serious," added Lydia. "Our differences just got in the way."

"Wait. So you guys don't get along anymore?"

"No but I'm working on it."

"That's why you haven't mentioned her name, or talked with her over the phone. I knew something wasn't right."

With her back facing her mother, leaning against the sink, Lydia stood in silence.

"But you're best friends...nothing should set you apart."

"I know." Lydia turned to face her mother. "Like I said, I'm working on it."

"Abigail's such a religious person, but I can't believe she's *not* the reason why you took an interest in reading the Bible."

"She was, but wasn't. I mean, not in the way you might be thinking." Lydia took a deep breath. "So this is what happened..."

Ruth sat down and propped her elbows on the table. She then rested her chin on her hands, listening to all Lydia had to say. Her brows shot up and down as Lydia gave her a recap as to what happened on the day she was working. She couldn't believe they argued as they did, especially in front of customers.

"...Anyways, when I left work, I walked to the bus stop. And as I waited for the bus, a homeless guy came up to me and asked for a quarter. But I gave him a dollar and then he left. Seconds later, he returned and gave me a pamphlet."

Lydia described what was on the cover, and how she felt sorry for the Sacrificed Lamb. Squinting her eyes, Ruth paid close attention to every word Lydia spoke. She made the connection of her daughter's day: the argument she had with Abigail, the homeless man who approached her, and the pamphlet he had given her—and how it motivated her to read the Bible. But Ruth wasn't able to make the connection when it came to the Lamb and the Bible.

Lydia giggled. "Don't feel bad, Mom. I was confused too. But when I read what was inside the pamphlet, it made sense." Lydia walked to the table and sat across from her mother. "I still have it, do you wanna see it?"

"Uh"—Ruth straightened her posture and pressed her back against the chair—"sure. Why not?"

Lydia jumped up from her chair and bumped her knee under the table. Her mother asked if she was all right, and Lydia nodded before she ran out of the kitchen and up the stairs. The bump caused her knee to throb, but she ignored the pain. Sharing her testimony with her mother, which led to her salvation, was more important than an aching limb.

CHAPTER 8

Lydia returned with the Lamb's story in one hand, and the Bible in the other. She handed it to her mother and watched as she studied it. After flipping through the pages, Ruth handed the pamphlet back to Lydia.

"In case you're wondering, the names on the back of the pamphlet belong to the strangers I met that day. The day Abigail and I had our argument. Daniel's the one who gave me the pamphlet."

"So who's Joshua?"

"The other homeless guy—Daniel's friend."

"Oh." Guilt and shame attacked Ruth once more. She realized she wasn't the only one in their neighborhood having a hard time.

"Do you mind if I read it to you?" asked Lydia.

"No. Go right ahead."

Ruth clasped her hands and rested them on her lap as Lydia read the story of *The Sacrificed Lamb*.

"...After reading this story, that's when I decided to give the Bible a try." Lydia set the pamphlet on the table and smiled. "Wasn't the story captivating?"

Ruth beamed. "Yes, it was."

"You know music isn't my only passion—I love stories too. Anyways, in the story of the Lamb, it mentions 'the book.' Meaning, the Bible. But I didn't understand some of the descriptions and symbolism, which is another reason why I wanted to check out the Bible. You know, to get a better understanding of everything I've read."

Lydia's explanation made it easy for Ruth to understand the purpose as to why she began reading the Bible. But it was her fervor that explained it all. Ruth was happy for her daughter's newfound faith, but it also made her feel alone. And even covetous for the hope she carried.

"...so at the end of the Lamb's story, I found out that he was actually—Jesus Himself."

"Fascinating, ha!" Ruth glowed with excitement, but then she winced. The pain from her sickness had struck again. She leaned into the table and rested her head on top of her folded arms.

"Are you ok, Mom?"

Ruth nodded, remaining in the same position.

Lydia walked over to her mother and laid a hand on her back. "Mom, I really want you to get well. And after reading a particular Scripture, over and over, it's really increased my faith."

"What are you implying?" Ruth moaned as the pain intensified.

"We've tried almost everything, right?" Lydia waited for a response, but her mother remained silent. "I don't know what else to do, which is why I went to the church for help."

Ruth slowly lifted her head up. "Honey, can you hand me my medications and a cup of water?"

Lydia did as she was asked, tears forming in her dispirited eyes.

"I appreciate your concern, honey," said Ruth, "but I don't feel comfortable having someone come here to pray for me."

"Mom, all you have to do is listen. Leave the praying to Pastor Paul, and to me."

Ruth raised a brow. "It sounds too easy. You sure nothing else is required?" Her mother's quizzical look was paired with a gentle smile. She seemed to be open-minded about God, the Bible...and perhaps prayer.

Lydia's shoulders relaxed, so did the wrinkles on her forehead.

"You, ok?" asked Ruth.

"Yeah." A smile tugged at the corner of Lydia's lips. "So, to answer your question—yes. There's *one* more thing required."

Ruth's eyes sparkled with intrigue. "Really? And what would that be?"

"Faith."

"But will faith be enough to cure my cancer?"

Lydia sat down and slumped back in her chair. The faith she had for her mother's healing was attacked with doubt. Her mother's questionable faith, or lack thereof, caused Lydia to consider her own.

"The pastor comes in and says something to my sickness—then *bam*, I'm healed! Is this what you think will happen?" Heat rose to Ruth's face. She was agitated by the idea of being cured by faith alone. She had relied on doctors and medications to rid her of the disease, but they had only brought temporary relief.

Tears gushed down Lydia's face. She was no longer able to hold back her emotions. But through her disappointment, she continued with their conversation. "I was skeptical at first too. But when I read the pamphlet Daniel gave me, it brought me hope. Even more so when I started reading the Bible."

Lydia picked up a napkin and wiped away at her tear-streaked face.

"I'm not sure how God does it, but I know He can heal you, Mom."

Overcome with an array of emotions, Ruth was unable to speak. Her lips quivered and then she wept.

"Mom, just 'cause you're sick, doesn't mean you have to claim it. It's in your body, but it doesn't have to stay there. All I'm asking, is to let Pastor Paul pray for you."

Ruth wiped her tears away with the back of her hand. "Maybe you're right." She stood from her chair and walked out of the kitchen.

Lydia furrowed her brows. What was her mother referring to? She jumped out of her chair and dashed up the stairs.

"Mom"—Lydia entered her mother's bedroom—"Are you ok?"

"Not really," replied Ruth.

Lydia walked over to the window and stood next to her mother. She placed an arm around her mother's shoulders, trying to comfort her as she sniffled. "Mom, what did you mean, when you said maybe I was right?"

"It was in reference to having a sickness that doesn't belong to me." Ruth pressed a hand against the window, her forehead following suit. "But it seems like I don't have a choice."

"But you do, Mom."

Ruth knew what her daughter meant. "I don't mind giving him a chance—so tell Pastor Paul he can come over."

Lydia hugged her. "Thanks, Mom. You're making the right decision."

"But do you think he'll come back? I was so rude to him."

"Don't worry, he will." Lydia gave her mother a kiss on the cheek.

"I hope your faith is big enough for the both of us. Because the stage I'm in, makes my healing seem like an impossibility."

"I don't care what stage you're in, Mom. I have faith for a miracle."

It was early in the afternoon when Lydia left the house. When she arrived at the church, nobody seemed to be around. But then her searching eyes landed on the church sign—Thursday's service wouldn't begin for another two hours. She let out a long sigh and headed back home.

On her way back, someone in a station wagon honked in the opposite direction she was headed. Lydia stole a glimpse, thinking it was meant for somebody else, but then another honk followed. The vehicle slowly pulled up next to her, and she slowed her pace, but remained cautious as the passenger side window rolled down. A smile of relief slid across Lydia's face—it was Grace, the secretary from church.

"Hi, honey, do you remember me?" Grace smiled as she leaned her head out the window.

"Yeah. You're the lady who works at the church. Front desk, right?"

Grace nodded. "That's right. Speaking of church, will you be joining us for today's service?"

"Funny you ask," said Lydia. "I just left the church since no one was there."

"That's because service starts at—"

"Two this afternoon," interrupted Lydia. "I saw the time on the church's sign."

Grace glanced down at her gold watch. "Which would be an hour and forty-five minutes from now."

"So what kind of service is it?" Lydia wondered if there was a difference between Sunday mornings and weekly services.

"We have praise and worship every Thursday."

"Oh." Lydia hesitated. "Do you think I'd be able to talk to Pastor Paul, then?"

"I'm sorry, honey, but the pastor is out of town."

Lydia frowned. "Oh, ok."

"Are you all right?"

"Yeah, I'm fine." Lydia lowered her head and walked away.

Grace put the car in park and got out. "Wait! Was Pastor Paul expecting you today?"

"No, but I was hoping he could pray for my mom."

"How is your mother doing?"

"About the same." The shimmer in Lydia's eyes faded as she envisioned her mother in pain.

"I know Pastor Paul paid you and your mother a visit," said Grace, "but I—"

4 44

"Sorry, I gotta go," said Lydia. "It was nice to see you again."

"Ok, honey, I'll let Pastor Paul know that you need his assistance." Grace knew she was upset, so she stayed put as Lydia walked off. "This is the grace of God given to you, so that you can be persistent in seeking His face. As king David said, 'I waited patiently for the Lord and He turned to me and heard my cry.'"

Lydia appreciated Grace's encouragement, but didn't have time to ponder its meaning.

"I'm sorry, honey"—Grace slid back into the station wagon, the driver's door slamming shut—"what's your name again?"

She came to a halt and turned around. "Lydia."

"God is faithful...remember that, Lydia." Grace waved as she drove away.

"See ya," whispered Lydia. She appreciated the encounter she had with Grace, but for some reason, it felt as if her faith drove off as well—in the opposite direction. If Pastor Paul couldn't see her mother in the next few days, she feared her mother would change her mind.

Ruth needed prayer, and she needed it now.

CHAPTER 9

G ood afternoon, Grace." Pastor Jonathan extended his hand.

"Hi, Pastor Jonathan." She smiled as she shook his hand. "Looks like we've arrived earlier than everyone else."

"We sure did." Pastor Jonathan grinned. "So, how have you been?"

"I'm doing wonderful, thank you. How about you?" Grace searched the perimeter with anxious eyes.

He followed her gaze. "I'm good. Is everything ok? You look concerned."

Grace turned her attention back on Pastor Jonathan. "I'm fine...just looking to see if the young girl I've been talking with was here."

"Is she part of the youth group?"

She shook her head. "No, she came by a couple weeks ago, seeking support for her sick mother." Grace worried if she was being discreet enough. She trusted Pastor Jonathan, but didn't want to say any more without Lydia's consent. "She's supposed to be here to speak with Pastor Paul."

"Oh, I see. What about today's service? Will she be attending it as well?"

"I hope so." Grace walked to the front entrance of the church and pulled the double doors open. "Let's get inside before we get rained on."

The sky darkened as storm clouds gathered over the church.

An elderly woman with a cane hobbled up the aisle. "Is that you, Pastor Jonathan?"

"Indeed it is." Pastor Jonathan smiled as he and Grace stood by the front entrance.

"Just wanted to make sure since my sight is declining." The grayed-haired woman stopped at the last set of pews, pushing her glasses up the bridge of her nose. "I'm so happy that we have young, spirit-filled pastors like you. That's what makes the church move forward, you know? Our lukewarm brothers and sisters need the fire of the Holy Ghost to ignite their hearts."

"Amen, sister," said Pastor Jonathan. "But it takes the whole congregation to accomplish this...and more."

"Hallelujah!" The elderly woman raised her cane in agreement.

With a little time to spare before service, Pastor Jonathan wanted to share something with the woman, including Grace. He asked the woman to take a seat as he and Grace sat in the pew right across from her. "As I was praying on my way to church, I had a vision in my spirit— I saw a young person crying out for help. It reminded me of Paul, from the Book of Acts, when he had a vision of a man begging him for help. My entire being felt heavy due to the intensity of what I saw. I believe God was giving me a message concerning the young generation, including the youths who attend this church. Even those He will lead here."

Grace raised her hands in gladness. "Praise the Lord for the insight He's given you." Her eyes widened as something came to mind. "Oh, Lord!" She turned to Pastor Jonathan, her hands cradling the sides of her face.

"What is it, Grace?"

"The girl in your vision...maybe it's the same girl I told you about."

Pastor Jonathan raised a brow. "The girl with the sick mother?"

"Yes. But I told her Pastor Paul is out of town." Grace sighed. "She looked really sad. Pastor Jonathan, would you please give her a call, and see if she is willing to let you pay a visit to her mother?"

A sympathetic smile slid across his face as Grace fumbled through her purse.

"Here's her number—just in case," said Grace.

Lydia wasn't ready to go home just yet. She wanted to bring her mother a miracle, but all she had was a fragment of hope. Stalling for time, she walked toward the neighborhood grocery store. Outside the entrance of Shalom, an elderly woman struggled with her malfunctioned shopping cart, dropping a few items onto the ground.

"Hi. Do you need some help?" asked Lydia.

The elderly woman looked up and beamed. "Ahh...you are a godsend, angel baby. I was so worried I wouldn't have anyone to help me load my groceries in the car. Thank you!"

"You're welcome." Lydia grinned as she took the cart. "Wow. This cart is rough."

"I'm telling you, angel baby, it has seen better days."

Lydia pushed and shoved, trying to avoid the bumps sprawled across the parking lot. *The shopping cart isn't the only thing who's seen better days*, thought Lydia as she barely made it to the woman's car.

After loading all the groceries, the woman asked Lydia for another favor. "Sorry to bother you, angel baby. But may I borrow your phone? I forgot mine at home and I need to call my grandson, making sure if he made it home yet. He's staying with me for the rest of this summer."

"I would, but I forgot mine too." Lydia frowned. "I'm sorry."

"No worries, angel baby. But how in the world did you forget it? It's rare to see a youngster like you without a phone." She chuckled.

"I know, right?" Lydia giggled. "I rarely forget it unless I'm in a hurry."

"Before I leave, let me ask you something." The woman pressed her back against the driver's door. "Does it feel like a part of you is missing when you don't have your phone?"

"Yeah...it does." A hint of pink flushed Lydia's face. "I use my phone 'cause I don't wanna feel disconnected from anyone, especially my mom. It gives me a sense of security, too, but it also consumes my time."

"I couldn't agree anymore. Most young folks always check this and that...."

"Which is why I'm gonna change my lifestyle."

The woman arched a brow. "How so, angel baby?"

"By using my phone for what really matters. You know, checking emails, schedules, and staying in touch with my mom and my best—"

"Friend?" interrupted the woman.

Lydia nodded. "Yeah."

"It's apparent you've been seeking wisdom." The woman's eyes lit up in admiration. "Good for you, angel baby."

"Thanks." Lydia's countenance appeared brighter due to the woman's compliment. "My mom says I'm calmer and more sensible than ever before."

The woman stepped away from her car. "Ok, angel baby, I best be going. Hope I didn't keep you too long. Talking is one of my weaknesses."

They both laughed.

"No, it's fine. I really enjoyed talking with you."

"I'm glad to hear that." The woman cocked her head to the side. "Forgive me for the delay, but what's your name?"

"Lydia."

"Well, Lydia, thank you so much for everything." She turned around and lifted up on the handle of the driver's door. "My name's Mary, by the way."

"Nice to meet you, Mary."

The woman slid into her car. "I believe we met for a greater reason than you helping me with my groceries."

Lydia nodded as she pondered Mary's statement.

Mary stepped out of the car. "Wait right there, Lydia." She walked around to the trunk and rummaged through the bags.

Did she forget to buy something at the store? thought Lydia.

"Would you please take this?" She held out a loaf of bread. "I usually get one for myself, but since this item is new, I decided to get two of them."

Lydia's shoulders tensed. "Thanks but I can—"

"Please, Lydia, I just want to say thank you."

"Are you sure? I mean, with your grandson coming and...."

"Absolutely. It's very hard to find a person like you, especially in this day and age. And don't worry, the Lord will bless what we have."

"Thank you." Lydia took the bread from Mary's hand.

"Don't mention it, angel baby. May the Lord bless you and grant all of your wishes." She got back into her car and spoke another blessing over Lydia before backing out.

Lydia whispered another "thank you" as Mary drove away.

CHAPTER 10

Grace and Jonathan were talking as the gate surrounding the church crept opened. They turned around and their eyes widened—an unexpected visitor walked toward them.

"Pastor Paul, what a surprise!" said Grace with a huge smile.

He tucked his Bible under his arm. "And hello to the both of you. How have you been, Grace?" Pastor Paul switched his gaze over to Jonathan. "And how about you?"

"Good," replied Grace.

"Same here," added Pastor Jonathan. "What a surprise to see you here. I thought you wouldn't be back until Saturday."

"So did I," replied Pastor Paul. "Some of the church leaders were not able to make it today due to personal reasons. Which is why I'm back earlier than expected."

"Were you able to address anything at the meeting during your time away?" asked Grace.

Pastor Paul nodded. "Before I was asked to return home, we had just passed some regulations and agendas. But the others will have to wait until our next meeting."

"Thank the Lord," replied Grace, "but you must be tired. You should have stayed at home to get some rest before coming here."

"I'm fine, just a little weary from the drive. Besides, I really feel the need to be here for tonight's service, which is why I came early so we can pray before everyone arrives." He directed his gaze to Jonathan. "I also sense that you need to give a particular message this evening. Are you sensing this too?"

"Yes." Pastor Jonathan nodded. "In fact, I was just sharing a special message with Grace—a vision that was recently revealed to me. But I'm not sure if the message is meant for a certain individual, or for the whole congregation."

Grace took over the conversation. "Jonathan told me he saw a person crying out for help, in his spirit."

"But it wasn't clear who I saw." Pastor Jonathan shrugged as Pastor Paul shifted from one foot to the other, paying close attention.

"Jonathan, I think I know who you saw," stated Grace. "Remember the girl I told you about earlier?"

"Yes. The girl with the sick mother," replied Pastor Jonathan.

"You mean Lydia?" asked Pastor Paul.

"That's right, Lydia," responded Grace. "I feel this could be the person the Lord revealed to Jonathan."

"Really?" Pastor Paul arced a brow. "By any chance, have you seen her? She and her mother are always in my daily prayers."

"I have!" Grace perked up. "I saw her today on my way to church, so I stopped to chat with her. She was on her way here to see you."

"Is Lydia ok? How about her mother?" Anxiousness took over Pastor Paul's voice, a worry line zigzagging across his forehead.

"From what I could tell, she looked fine. Really, she did." Grace gave Pastor Paul a reassuring smile. "She just looked disappointed more than anything when I told her you were out of town."

"I wonder if her mother changed her mind." Pastor Paul's eyes glossed over as he recollected the day he paid Lydia and her mother a visit.

"I've been wondering the same," replied Grace. "Since we didn't expect you back so soon, I told Jonathan about Lydia. And I gave him her phone number, so he could speak with her. But I didn't give him any details, I wanted it to come from Lydia."

"Good thinking, Grace," said Pastor Paul. "So did you give her a call already, Jonathan?"

Pastor Jonathan shook his head. "No, not yet. We were talking about Lydia just before you arrived."

"Ok. I'll give her a call then," said Pastor Paul. "Will you two join me in prayer before I do so?"

"Hello," said a familiar voice.

"Hi. May I speak to Lydia please?" requested Pastor Paul.

"Who is this?"

"This is Pastor Paul." He knew he was speaking to Ruth, so he repeated, "Can I speak to Lydia?"

"She is not available. How can I help you?"

Pastor Paul wrinkled his forehead. He didn't expect Ruth to answer the phone, and he had no idea how to respond to her last question. Not knowing if she knew her daughter had reached out to the church again, Pastor Paul was concerned how she might react to his reason for calling, so he looked over at Grace and Jonathan for help. Their reassuring smiles and encouraging gestures gave him the confidence to proceed.

"I just wanted to check up on you and Lydia. I hope that's ok."

Ruth hesitated then replied, "We're fine."

"That's good to hear." Pastor Paul wanted to believe her, but a part of him said otherwise. "And if you ever need anything, I'm just a phone call away. Hope you have a blessed afternoon."

"You too. And, Pastor Paul, I'm sorry I offended you the last time we spoke."

His eyes widened. "Thank you but no need to apologize. I totally understand where you were coming from."

"Thanks." Ruth smiled. "And by the way, have you met up with Lydia?"

"I have, but it's been a while." Pastor Paul still didn't want to disclose why he was calling since their conversation was going so smooth.

"Really? I thought the two of you met up today?"

"I haven't seen anyone besides the church staff since arriving home."

"So you were out of town?"

"Yes, for a meeting. But Grace, our church secretary, informed me about Lydia heading to the church earlier today."

"Do you know where she headed afterwards?" Ruth's heart rate sped up as her stomach twisted.

"I'm not sure."

Pastor Paul told Ruth to hold on, so he could ask Grace if she knew where Lydia might have gone after they talked. But Grace shrugged her shoulders, telling him she didn't know. Concern etched their faces, including Pastor Jonathan's.

"Wherever she may have gone," said Pastor Paul, "I'm sure she's on her way back home."

"I hope so." Ruth fought against her troublesome thoughts, believing Lydia was all right and that she would be walking through the front door any minute.

A few minutes later, Lydia walked into the house. "Hey, Mom."

"You're ok!" Ruth got to her as quick as she could, wrapping her arms around her. "You forgot your phone."

"I know. Sorry to worry you." Lydia was trapped inside her mother's embrace.

Ruth released her arms around Lydia. "I gave you a call, but then I heard your phone ringing—it was on the table."

"Go figure, the day I forget my phone, everyone wants to contact me. Or ask to use it."

"Who wanted to use your phone?"

"A sweet old lady at the grocery store. Which is why I was late getting back home."

"What did she need it for?"

"To make sure her grandson made it home all right." Lydia headed to the kitchen.

Ruth followed her. "What's in the bag?"

"Lunch." Lydia placed the bag on the table.

"Oh, honey. You are too thoughtful. First you make us breakfast, and next you bring us lunch." She gave Lydia another hug along with a kiss on the cheek.

"You're welcome, Mom. I wanted to make veggie sandwiches, but we needed bread and a tomato, so I stopped by Shalom on my way back home."

"Sounds delicious." Ruth placed a hand on her growling stomach. "But we could've done without the bread. Remember, I want you to save your money."

"It's fine, Mom. The money I spent won't affect what I'm saving for school." Lydia reached into the bag. "Plus, the lady I met gave me this loaf of bread."

Ruth's eyes sparkled with gratitude. "How kind of her!"

"I know." Lydia smiled. "She wanted to repay me for loading her car with groceries, so that's why it took me longer to get home, including the conversation we had about cell phones."

Ruth pulled out a chair and sat at the table while Lydia made their sandwiches.

"She complimented me about seeking wisdom, and then asked if I read the Bible," continued Lydia.

"And what did you tell her?"

"That I started reading the Bible not too long ago."

Ruth nodded her head as she processed all her daughter had said. "It's easy for a person to recognize someone else who does something similar, which can include one's demeanor and personality traits."

"Good point, Mom." Lydia's face lit up. "She told me she started reading the Bible around my age."

"There you go." Ruth reached toward Lydia and rested a hand on her arm. "I can see the change in you as well. But can you?"

Lydia furrowed a brow. "The change? As in changing because I'm reading the Bible?"

"Uh-huh."

"I don't know." Lydia shrugged. "But if Abigail and I were still friends, I'm sure she would."

"Meaning?"

"Meaning, you know how serious Abigail is in her faith. And how she would notice something like that."

"She could very well be the driving force behind it"— she looked Lydia straight in the eyes—"your transformation, that is."

"Maybe." Lydia picked up her sandwich and then put it down. "Who am I kidding? Abigail is *totally* the reason why. I always got annoyed when she talked to me about God and the Bible, but now...here I am doing the same."

"But that's a good thing."

"Mom, do you believe things happen for a reason?"

"I believe there's always consequences that follow our choices. But, I do believe certain things are meant to happen—no matter what."

Lydia's mouth dropped open. Where did her mother's unexpected faith come from? Surely it wasn't from her, or from Pastor Paul. Or was it?

CHAPTER 11

H e's on his way," said Ruth.

"What are you talking about?" asked Lydia. "Who's on his way?"

"The pastor you brought to the house a few weeks ago."

Lydia remained silent as she stared at her mother in wonderment.

"I know where you went the other day." Ruth took a breath and continued, "And it wasn't just to the grocery store."

"You knew I went to see—"

"Pastor Paul," interrupted Ruth. "While you were at Shalom, he called to check up on us."

"But how did he know I wanted to talk to him? On my way to church, I spoke to Grace, and she said he was out of town."

"He was, but his meeting was cut short, so he arrived back home that same day. Anyhow, Grace told him you wanted to speak to him, so that's why he called."

"Wait...what?" Lydia threw her arms up, her palms facing upward. "'Cause the last time he was here—"

"I was rude, but I apologized when he called."

"You did?"

Ruth snickered at Lydia's unbelief. "Yes, I really did."

"So what did he—"

The door bell rang.

"Get the door, Lydia, it might be him."

Lydia sucked in a deep breath as she twisted the front door open. Her brows rose and her heart raced. She knew who the visitor on the left was, but to the one on the right, she had no clue who he was. Or why he was here. She swallowed the lump in her throat and forced a smile, switching her gaze between Pastor Paul and his friend—Pastor Jonathan.

"Hi, Lydia," said Pastor Paul.

"Uh...hi." She looked over her shoulder and stared at her mother in disbelief. Ruth smiled and gave her daughter a squeeze to the arm, reassuring her that she was not dreaming. Lydia turned her attention back on their guests.

"Surprised to see me?" Pastor Paul chuckled.

"Uh...I...yeah." Lydia cleared her throat. "My mom said you were coming over, but Grace told me you were out of town."

"I was, but our meeting came to a close sooner than anticipated." Pastor Paul gestured to the right. "Lydia, Ruth, I'd like for you to meet Pastor Jonathan. He's one of the youth pastors in our church."

"Hi, Lydia, it's nice to meet you," said Pastor Jonathan, "and you as well, ma'am."

Lydia smiled as her mother shook hands with the youth pastor.

"Grace said she spoke with you on your way to church today," stated Pastor Paul. "And she mentioned you wanted to speak with me. So, that's why I'm here"—he looked over at Pastor Jonathan—"why we're here."

"Yeah, I did. I was gonna ask if you would pray for my mom again." Lydia glanced to her right, where her mother stood at her side.

"Sorry to keep the two of you waiting," interjected Ruth. "Please, come in."

Lydia and her mother stepped aside as the pastors walked into their home. Ruth gestured to the full-length couch where the two men took a seat. And as for Ruth, she sat down in her rocking chair as Lydia claimed a spot on the love seat.

"How are you doing, Ruth?" inquired Pastor Paul. He felt honored to be among Lydia and Ruth once again, especially since their first encounter did not go as planned.

"Despite the pain and sickness, I'm ok." Ruth thought about her mythical beliefs of healing and miracles before continuing. "I'm glad you're here, Pastor Paul. You, too, Pastor Jonathan."

Pastor Paul could not afford to waste a second concerning this golden opportunity, so he immediately jumped into his mission. "If it's ok with you, Ruth, could we talk a little bit about the Word of God?"

Ruth's lips tightened in a straight line. "That's fine. But please, keep it as basic as possible. I get overwhelmed with too much information."

The creaking sound of Ruth's rocking chair echoed through the living room as Pastor Paul opened his Bible. Pastor Jonathan took his Smartphone out to follow along. When he began to read, a tear slid down Lydia's face, but she quickly wiped it away. Her mother was a strong woman, so she didn't want to make her uncomfortable by being emotional. For Ruth had given Pastor Paul a second chance to come over, and Lydia didn't want anything to get in the way, which included her.

"The circumstances that you are facing right now are very immense. But I assure you, it is never bigger than our Lord; rather it is like chaff before the wind," said Pastor Paul. "Most of the time, our problems seem impossibly large, but they're not. For greater is He who is in us, than he who is in the world."

The creaking of Ruth's rocking chair came to a halt. She fixed her eyes on Pastor Paul, contemplating all he had said.

"Not every problem stems from ourselves," continued Pastor Paul. "Some of them are the results from the mistakes and sins of others, but when it comes to the enemy of our souls, he's always throwing problems our way. But the ones that do come from us, there is good news! The Bible says in first John 'If we confess our sins, he is faithful and just and will forgive us our sins and purify us from all unrighteousness.' Sometimes we humans assume that if we do a good deed or attend church on a regular basis—we're doing God a favor along with making up for our wrong doings. But the truth is, God is all about forming intimate relationships with His children: 'He has told you, O man, what is good. And what does the LORD require of you? To act justly and to love mercy and to walk humbly with your God.'"

Lydia looked at her mother, wondering if the solemn expression on her face was one of disbelief, or one of boredom. But it was neither. Ruth was still processing every word that Pastor Paul had spoken to her. Both pastors were able to discern what was happening inside her heart—Ruth was being convicted of her sins by the Holy Ghost.

"Ruth, please allow me to pray for you, to invite the Lord Jesus into your life," said Pastor Paul. "Just like I did for Lydia."

Ruth sighed and looked away. She rocked back and forth in her chair, staring out the window. Again, everyone wondered what she was thinking. Her lack of response made Pastor Paul think he had offended her somehow. Lydia and Pastor Jonathan thought this as well, but they were wrong—she was more than ready to receive a miracle.

Ruth wanted to live...not just survive.

"Ok," said Ruth, "you can pray for me." She turned her head and looked Pastor Paul in the eyes. "I love my daughter more than anything...I'll do whatever it takes to always be here for her."

Ruth was deeply moved by the Scriptures Pastor Paul read from the Bible. They were powerful and convicting. But so was the way he had elaborated the Word of God, making it easier for her to understand the repercussions of sin, whether intentional or not, and the deception of rectifying one's disobedience by doing good deeds. Ruth, however, thought the only way to be healed was through a mythical requirement—salvation. Which is why she agreed to have Pastor Paul lead her through prayer. She did believe, but she was also skeptical.

Pastor Paul bowed his head and led Ruth in prayer. "Dear Lord Jesus, I know I am a sinner and I ask You to forgive my sins."

Ruth followed, repeating each word at a slow pace.

"...I thank you for giving me this opportunity," continued Pastor Paul. "In Jesus's name. Amen." After the prayer of repentance, Pastor Paul asked Ruth if he could continue praying for her and Lydia. She nodded, bowed her head, and closed her eyes once again.

"Lord, I thank you very much for my sister's redemption, and now I ask for the bread of healing that you have provided for your children. We receive this not because we deserve it, but because of Your mercy, grace, and goodness that endures forever." Pastor Paul laid his hand on Ruth's shoulder as he placed another hand on top of Lydia's head. "Dear Lord, I bless this child who is looking up to Your miraculous hands. I ask You to answer her prayer by showing her that You are always with her. And that You are not a respecter of persons. Please stir her talent for the glory of Your kingdom. In your wonderful and miracle-working name, I pray. Amen."

Everyone lifted their heads and opened their eyes. Ruth's face was soaked in tears and so was Lydia's. Pastor Paul and Pastor Jonathan were teary-eyed as well. Ruth reached for the box of tissues sitting on the windowsill and pulled out a few before handing them over to Lydia.

Pastor Paul spoke words of encouragement over Ruth and Lydia as they wiped their tears away. "...and whatever things we ask in prayer, believing, we will receive."

In unison, everyone said, "Amen!"

Ruth's countenance was gleaming with relief and assurance. She stood up from her rocking chair and walked over to Pastor Paul and Pastor Jonathan. "I thank the both of you for coming."

"Oh, thank you," responded Pastor Paul. "We are so grateful to have been invited to your home. Most importantly, for inviting the Lord into your life. Ruth, nothing should ever stand between you and the Lord—for everything in this life will pass away. Therefore, securing our eternal destination is the most important thing we can do."

Ruth and Lydia smiled as they nodded their agreement.

"Gentlemen, would you like some coffee or tea?" asked Ruth.

"Thank you, but we must leave now," replied Pastor Paul. "Our afternoon service will begin very soon."

Ruth looked over at the wall clock. "Oh, my. I didn't realize how much time has passed."

Two hours had gone by.

"No apology needed," said Pastor Paul. "We would stay longer if we could. With that said, service starts at two o'clock, and we would love for you and Lydia to join us." He switched his gaze over to Lydia. "And feel free to invite your friends."

"What a wonderful idea," said Ruth. "Lydia has a best friend who would be more than happy to attend."

Lydia cleared her throat, very loud. Ruth looked over at her and realized she should have refrained from making her last comment. For a brief moment, she had forgotten that the girls were not getting along.

"You know what, we'll give you a call, and let you know if we can make it or not," added Ruth. "I think Lydia may have to go into work today."

Both pastors could sense something was off, but they didn't want to come off as pushy, so they kept quiet and smiled their understanding. Next, everyone followed Ruth to the front door where handshakes, thanksgiving, and smiles were exchanged. Ruth opened the door and the two men walked away. But then, Pastor Paul came to a halt and glanced over his shoulder. "Lydia, I believe the Lord will bring out your talent to glorify His name."

Lydia's eyes twinkled with hope as she and her mother stood in the doorway.

Lydia and her mother had kindly declined Pastor Paul's invitation—they were not ready to be around a room full of other believers, and Lydia was not ready to make amends with Abigail. Besides that, Lydia was adjusting at a rapid pace when it came to reading her Bible on a daily basis along with praying and asking for prayer. But Ruth had only begun to open herself up to God, and His Word. Having Pastor Paul and Pastor Jonathan visit their home was a huge leap of faith in itself.

So, they stayed home and continued to converse. They made their way to the kitchen and sat at the table. Their topic of choice was inspired by Pastor Paul's last statement before he and Pastor Jonathan headed to church.

"He's right," said Ruth, "you're very talented."

Lydia beamed. "Thanks, Mom. But do you believe God will actually use me for a greater purpose?"

"Absolutely." Ruth smiled. "I was hard on you at first, too hard actually, about you trying out for the singing contest. My fear for you got in the way, not knowing if you'd make it or not. You deserve to be a star, Lydia, but not on my account."

"I love you more than anything, Mom. But winning a singing contest and everything that comes with fame, will never be a priority." Lydia's eyes shimmered with tears as she took hold of her mother's hand. "Your healing and good health is all that matters."

Ruth squeezed Lydia's hand as a happy tear slid down her face. "We may not have much, but we'll always have each other."

CHAPTER 12

D ays had gone by since Pastor Paul had invited Lydia and Ruth to their weekly service. This discussion, however, was brought up again. Ruth tried her best to convince Lydia to reach out to Abigail, knowing their friendship was too precious, even priceless, to throw away due to their differences. Not only that, but Ruth wanted Lydia to continue on the path she was going, and she was certain Abigail would encourage her to do so.

Lydia huffed. "Ok, I'll try."

"There is nothing to try," replied Ruth. "Abigail is a devoted Christian and I don't think she would refuse your invitation."

"Mom, just because I'm a Christian now—doesn't mean it'll solve the issues we have."

"Well, the only way to find out, is to give her a call."

Lydia rolled her eyes. "I'll think about it."

"Well, don't take too long. Because if one allows too much time to go by, it can prevent them from doing the right thing. Trust me, honey, I'm a perfect example of this."

Lydia struggled with the conversation she and her mother had about Abigail. It didn't have anything to do with valuing her mother's advice, but it was more like she needed a confirmation before giving her best friend, if she could still consider her that, a call. And the person who came to mind—was Pastor Paul.

She grabbed her Bible and flipped through the pages, looking for his number. A laugh escaped her when she found it nestled inside the book of Numbers. She pulled out her cell phone from the back pocket of her jeans and dialed away.

"Hello?" answered Pastor Paul.

"Hey, it's Lydia."

"Well hello, Lydia, how are you?" His kindness traveled through the air waves, making her feel at ease.

"I was wondering if you have time to talk...I need some advice."

Pastor Paul's face lit up. "Your timing is perfect. Rather, God's timing is perfect." He chuckled. "I just started my lunch break, how can I help you?"

"It's about my best friend." Lydia frowned then sighed. "Ex best friend, more like it."

"So tell me about—what's her name?"

"Abigail. And we had a major argument a few weeks ago. We haven't spoken since."

"I see." Pastor Paul propped an elbow on his desk and rested his chin on his hand. "When it comes to resolving arguments with those closest to us, they tend to be harder, creating more hurt and animosity."

Lydia nodded in agreement. "Tell me about it. At the time, we didn't see eye to eye about the singing contest. She didn't agree with my decision to try out, she basically told me seeking the world for help wasn't the answer to my problems. But I was just trying to make it to nationals, hoping to win, so I could support my mother financially."

"Aha. I remember when you and I had a similar conversation." He paused. "Can you hold on, for just a minute?"

"Yeah, sure."

Pastor Paul took a moment of silence as he sought the Holy Ghost for guidance as what to say next. He recalled this was the *same* friend she had mentioned before, and being he would have to consider both perspectives, he wanted to be fair yet sensitive toward Lydia.

"From a Christian perspective, Abigail is right about *not* seeking the world for answers, support, and so on. But, the Lord knows your reasoning as to why you wanted to enter the singing contest. He knows you did it out of love, and He will honor you for that. And Lydia, God is always faithful—He will take care of your mother, providing everything she needs, including what you need."

Lydia sniffled as tears ran down her face. "Thanks. I really needed to hear that."

"You're so welcome. As for Abigail, I believe she was coming from a good place. I can feel it in my spirit."

"Yeah, I guess you're right." Lydia blew out a sigh. "No. You're totally right. Abigail really cared about me...every little detail about my life, actually. Even my spiritual life, or lack thereof at the time."

"So I assume Abigail's a Christian as well?"

"Oh, yeah. A totally devoted and zealous one, at that."

Pastor Paul's smile reached his eyes. "Everything makes more sense now: Abigail's responses concerning the contest, which led to the argument the two of you had...."

He then went silent as the Holy Ghost fell upon him. Everything became much more clear, and he knew the words he needed to speak next—the very ones Lydia needed to hear.

"As a father, it's apparent Abigail is being raised in a biblical manner. Just as my wife and I are raising our sixteen-year-old son. The Bible says, 'Train up a child in the way he should go, and when he is old he will not depart from it.' My son is competent to make his own choices, and we have no control over his day to day tasks at school, or whenever he goes to have fun with his friends on the weekends. And just because I'm a pastor, it doesn't automatically make our son a Christian—he made that choice for himself. It's also his choice and responsibility to pursue his personal relationship with the Lord along with walking out his salvation."

Pastor Paul cleared his throat and then reached for the water bottle sitting on his desk.

"I meant to ask you this earlier, but what church does your friend go to?"

"Uh...I don't remember."

"No worries. It just dawned on me that we have a young lady who attends our youth group, whose name happens to be Abigail as well. And since we live in a small town, it wouldn't surprise me if —"

"She's the same girl who attends the youth group at your church," interrupted Lydia.

"Precisely." Pastor Paul chuckled. "So with all that said, it would be wonderful if the two of you could attend this week's youth group. You'd both be in good company, which could help break the ice as the both of you resolve your issues. True friends are hard to find, and I have a feeling your friendship with Abigail is worth saving."

"You're right. But I hope it's not too late. I've disrespected Abigail one too many times, not caring what she had to say along with hurting her feelings. Hopefully she'll forgive me."

"With the Lord, it's never too late."

Pastor Paul encouraged Lydia with Scriptures pertaining to friendship and forgiveness. And it worked! Lydia laughed as she recalled the fun and silly moments she and Abigail shared. This made Pastor Paul laugh with joy as well. He was deeply touched when Lydia told him about the advice her mother had given her concerning

Abigail. For it appeared that Ruth was softening up even more, realizing the value and importance of relationships along with giving her daughter sound advice.

"If you don't mind me asking, how old is your friend?" asked Pastor Paul.

"Eighteen."

"Well, how about that? The Abigail who attends our youth group is the same age as your friend. I'm pretty convinced that she most certainly is the same girl we're talking about."

Lydia giggled. "What a coincidence that would be."

"When it comes to God, there are no coincidences. Lydia, remember what I told you about God having a better plan for you?"

"Yeah."

"Well, I think Abigail is part of that glorious plan."

CHAPTER 13

It was lunchtime and Ruth was chowing down her meal. Lydia scrunched her face up, wondering where her mother mustered up such an appetite. It's been a long time since her mother ate without showing existing signs or symptoms of her sickness. Ruth also took her time when eating her meals, but not today.

"How was it, Mom?" asked Lydia.

"Well, I ate more than I usually do."

"That's an understatement." Lydia giggled. "I guess it means you're feeling good—like really good."

Ruth smiled. "I'm feeling all right."

When they had finished eating, Lydia took their plates and cups, and then walked over to the kitchen sink. After Lydia washed and dried them, she grabbed some plastic wrap and walked back to the table. She then picked up the bread, her eyes rounding in shock. She didn't realize it was made of whole wheat flour—and her mother had eaten it without having a reaction to its high-gluten content. Every time she consumed a gluten product, she immediately manifested intense painful reactions that persisted for hours.

"Oh my God!" Lydia dropped the bread and fled from the kitchen into the living room. She crouched down in front of the rocking chair and gazed up into her mother's eyes, guilt consuming every fiber of her being.

Ruth wrinkled her forehead as she stared down at Lydia. "What's wrong, honey? You're scaring me."

"I'm fine." Lydia's voice shook with apprehension. "The question is, are you?"

"Of course I'm fine. Why wouldn't I be?"

Lydia sighed with relief. "I shouldn't have used the bread I made your sandwich with. It has gluten in it."

"Really?" Ruth sat back in her rocking chair, wondering why she wasn't feeling sick.

"I'm so sorry, Mom." Lydia took her mother's hand and squeezed it. "I should have read the contents before making our lunch."

"No need to apologize, honey. I'm fine. Really, I am." Ruth patted the top of Lydia's head with her free hand.

"Come to think of it, I feel better than I have in a long time."

Lydia lifted her head and smiled up at her mother. "Maybe it's the beginning of God answering our prayers."

"Maybe." Ruth smiled back.

"I can't wait to share this good news with Pastor—oh, my goodness!"

"What? What's wrong now?"

Lydia straightened. "Mom, I didn't see you take your nausea medicine before we ate lunch."

Ruth followed suit. "Oh, my goodness! You're right."

"How could you forget?"

"I have no idea." Ruth jogged her memory. "Guess my hunger overshadowed my alertness."

"Yeah, you practically devoured your sandwich in one bite."

Ruth rolled her eyes. "I wouldn't say that."

"Are you kidding me? I thought you were gonna eat the plate too."

"Now that's a little extreme, don't you think?" Ruth arched a brow.

Lydia arched a brow in return. "Does it look like I'm kidding?"

Ruth smirked playfully and then turned to look at the wall clock. "At least our somber conversation has moved forward for the better, but as for the time, not so much. Didn't you change the battery in the clock yesterday?"

"Yeah, as soon as you asked me to."

"Hm?" Ruth stared at the clock, feeling perplexed. "What a strange day this has been."

"I know, right? But it's also been a good day. A REALLY good day."

Ruth nodded. "I'd be a fool to argue otherwise."

Lydia giggled as her mother took the clock off the wall to inspect it.

Ruth frowned. "I don't get it. The battery looks new."

"'Cause it is."

"Guess they're defected, then." Ruth headed to the kitchen with the clock. "Can you check your phone and tell me what time it is?"

Lydia followed her into the kitchen. "It's almost four o'clock."

Ruth opened the kitchen drawer and stared at her medications. "And this day keeps getting stranger."

"What do you mean?"

"Not only did I forget to take my nausea medication, but I forgot to take the other ones too."

Lydia rushed to her mother's side. "What! Are you going to be ok, Mom?"

"I'm fine, honey, just calm down."

"Ok, but the second you start feeling sick, I'm calling your doctor."

"No need to. It's almost time for my next dose. But I'm not sure if I'll take them or not."

"Mom, you have to!" Lydia paled. "You'll get sick if you don't."

"Are you sure about that? I haven't taken any of my medications today, and I feel better than I have in a long time."

Lydia raised her brows. "Guess our prayers have been answered?"

"I hope so." Ruth smiled a lopsided grin.

A few moments later, Lydia went upstairs to have some alone time with the Lord. She grabbed her Bible off the nightstand and knelt down in front of her window. As she praised the Lord for protecting her mother from eating the gluten-filled bread, Ruth was still downstairs, rummaging through the junk drawer for another battery, a battle taking place in her mind at the same time. A part of Ruth believed God was at work in her healing, at least for the day. But the other half of her heart was hijacked by unbelief.

Ruth woke up early the next morning and saw Lydia sleeping in a fetal position at the edge of her bed. Lydia refused to leave her mother's room since she opted *not* to take her medications after dinner last night. But Ruth didn't feel the need to since her body had responded so well without taking them all day yesterday.

A gentle smile slid across her face as she covered Lydia with her blanket. She got out of bed, making sure not wake Lydia, and then walked to the window. Rays of hope welcomed her as the rising sun peeked over the tree line. She had so much to be grateful for, and forgetting to take her medicine yesterday, was a blessing in disguise. But today, was even more of a blessing—Ruth couldn't believe her body was still free from pain and sickness.

Ruth was startled out of her reverie as Lydia grumbled, tossing around on the bed. She turned around and lunged forward, just in time, nudging Lydia further onto the bed with outstretched arms.

Lydia's eyes shot open. "What just...where am I?"

"You're in my room." Ruth laughed. "And you almost fell off the bed. But I saved you."

"Way to go, Mom." Lydia struggled to sit up, the blanket tangled around her legs. "How do you feel?"

"Surprisingly, better than yesterday."

"Really?"

"Really." Ruth twisted and pulled on the blanket, setting Lydia free.

Lydia sat up and threw her arms around her mother's neck. "That's so awesome!"

"It truly is." Ruth slid out from her daughter's embrace and held out a hand. "Come on, it's time to get up. I don't want you to be late for work."

"Work. Right." Lydia stretched and yawned before getting out of bed.

"I'll go make something for breakfast while you get ready."

"It's ok, Mom, I'll it make myself."

"No, I insist. Plus, I can give the doctor a call while I'm in the kitchen."

"Why?" Lydia's brows pinched together. "Are you feeling sick again?"

"Not at all." Ruth gave her a reassuring smile. "Promise."

"So why the phone call?"

"To set up an appointment. I can't wait to tell my doctor how good I'm feeling. I don't want get my hopes too high, but maybe the cancer is going away."

Lydia beamed. "The Bible says with God—all things are possible."

With that, Lydia showered and got ready for work. She then went downstairs and ate breakfast, and before she left, she reminded her mother to take her medications if she started to feel sick. Ruth reassured her that she would be fine, and if she needed anything, the doctor was only a phone call away. But that wasn't good enough for Lydia. She made her mother promise to give her a call as well. No matter if she blew up her phone all day. Ruth agreed and then she walked Lydia to the front door. She smiled and waved as Lydia walked down the sidewalk. Then, she shut the door and picked up her phone.

"Hi, I'd like to make an appointment with Doctor Luke."

"Are you having an emergency, ma'am?" asked the receptionist.

"No, but I do need a checkup."

"Ok, ma'am, let me check the calendar. I'll be back shortly."

"All right, thank you." Ruth poured herself another cup of coffee as she waited.

"Ma'am, I'm going to put you on the schedule for Monday at two o'clock.

Will this work for you?"

"Sounds perfect, thank you. See you then."

Ruth hung up the phone and brought the coffee mug up to her lips. She closed her eyes as she inhaled the spicy scent of cinnamon creamer.

"Hey, Mom. How ya doin'?"

"Fine. Just like I was thirty minutes ago." Ruth snickered.

"Did you take your medications?"

"No, honey, I didn't."

Lydia huffed. "Mom, I've been thinking, so just hear me out."

Ruth rocked back and forth in her rocking chair. "Go on."

"I don't wanna sound like a hypocrite, but I don't think it's safe to stop taking your medications."

"And this came to you since the last time we talked?"

Lydia pressed her lips together, feeling frustrated. "Remember the older lady I met at the grocery store the other day?"

"Uh-huh."

"And remember the compliment she gave me? About me seeking wisdom."

"I do."

"Well, I think we should use wisdom concerning your medications. Even though you've been feeling good, I think you should take them until your doctors appointment."

"I hear you, honey. And don't worry, I'll take them after we get off the phone."

"Oh, thank God! I was worried you'd get upset with me. And I wouldn't blame you if you did."

"It's fine. Now get back to work before you get in trouble."

"Ok, love you!"

"Love you too."

Ruth exhaled a deep breath as she continued to rock her chair in a slow manner. It was true—Lydia was wise for her age. And her mother was more than pleased how quick she was maturing, including in her spiritual life. She also acknowledged the amount of wisdom and knowledge Lydia had accumulated over the summer. But Ruth also discerned that her daughter's faith was being challenged when it came to her sickness. For she, too, was being challenged. Not as severe as Lydia was, however.

There was no denying that God had been involved with Ruth's health for the past two days. Still, it all seemed too good to be true.

CHAPTER 14

Lydia had requested to take the day off from work, so she could accompany her mother to her doctors appointment. After they arrived at the doctor's office, Ruth checked in and then they took a seat in the waiting room. Several minutes later, one of the nurses escorted them to an examining room where Ruth's vitals were checked—her temperature...blood pressure—along with taking some blood samples. Ruth sat on the examining table while Lydia remained seated in the chair right next to her mother as the nurse left the room to get Doctor Luke.

Ruth rubbed her hands together as her chest rose and fell at a rapid pace. As for Lydia, she stared at the floor, swinging her feet back and forth. Before they left the house, they had prayed for peace and for a favorable outcome. But now, their nerves were getting the best of them, so they decided to pray again. Lydia got up and stood next to her mother, getting ready to pray with her, but then someone knocked on the door.

The door gently opened and Doctor Luke walked in. He greeted them with a soothing and comforting voice along with a friendly smile. Their nerves settled as relief took over. Lydia continued to hold her mother's hand as he pulled up Ruth's EMR (Electronic Medical Record) on the computer.

"You look great, Ruth! How are you feeling?" asked Doctor Luke.

Ruth beamed. "Thank you. I feel great, actually."

"So, what brings you to the office today? You're not due for another checkup just yet."

"I know, but I wanted to talk to you about my recent health changes." Ruth drew in a long breath, afraid of his reaction. "For the past few days, I haven't been taking my medications. And I haven't felt better than I do now."

Doctor Luke raised a brow, his arms crossing over his chest. "Interesting. Please, tell me more about these changes, and why you have discontinued your medications—without seeking me first. Ruth, you know better. It is very dangerous to stop, or to modify, one's health plan without consulting their physician first."

His voice was firm yet laced with concern like a loving father's. Nonetheless, Ruth slumped her shoulders and lowered her head like a child who had just been scolded. Lydia's heart plummeted to her stomach, feeling her mother's shame and discomfort. Worst yet, Lydia was angry that her mother lied to her, telling her she had taken her medications when she didn't. She sank in her chair and frowned as guilt overcame her.

I should have left work and stayed on to my mom about taking her medications.

"The pain and aches have subsided drastically, so has the exhaustion. It's enabled me to get up and move around without struggling, or asking my daughter for help. I've had the energy to do light tasks around the house as well."

Ruth glanced up at Lydia and felt an onslaught of guilt and tears.

"To answer your next question, Doctor Luke, I haven't been taking them because of forgetting to. And when I had realized this, I also realized I didn't feel sick. So, I wanted to test it out by skipping my next dose, which led me to skip the others...."

Doctor Luke's eyes gleamed with intrigue. "I'm at a loss for words. This rarely happens when a patient stops taking their medications."

Ruth nodded with a solemn expression. "Which is why I wanted to have an examination, hoping to get answers as to why I'm feeling better, instead of feeling worse."

Doctor Luke shifted from one foot to the other, stroking his chin. "Let me get this straight—you missed your medications on Thursday afternoon, all day Friday, and over the weekend too?"

"Yes," said Ruth matter-of-factly.

"And what about today?"

Ruth gulped. "No, I didn't take them today either."

His jaw tightened.

"Not only that, but I accidentally ate bread with gluten in it." A lopsided grin slid across Ruth's face.

Doctor Luke's nostrils flared out in frustration, and before he had a chance to respond, Lydia jumped to her feet and spoke up.

"It was my fault, though," said Lydia. "I should have checked the ingredients before making our sandwiches."

"But don't worry, Doctor Luke, nothing happened after I ate it," added Ruth.

"Ruth, you have been my patient for a long time, and I thought we've established a mutual respect and trust for one another. You have to be mindful of everything you eat, including consulting me when you make decisions pertaining to your health and well-being."

"I know. And I'm so sorry for being irresponsible"—Ruth closed her eyes and steadied her breathing, hoping the flood of emotions would subside—"but I'm telling you the truth, I honestly believe the medications have been making things worse. All I'm asking, is for you to give me an examination, so we can all know what's causing me to feel better."

Ruth sniffled as tears swam in her eyes.

"And if the test results prove that my healing is due to the medications, then I'll continue to take them, as long as I need to. But, if they prove otherwise...."

Doctor Luke was skeptical about Ruth's insinuation of receiving a so-called miracle. For centuries, there had always been rumors of people being healed in unexplainable and mysterious ways. Especially in the medical field. But Doctor Luke shook such possibilities from his mind.

"You know it's very important that your mother takes her medications, right?" asked Doctor Luke.

Lydia glanced over at her mother, her face etched with uncertainty, which made Ruth very upset.

"This is between you and me. So please leave my daughter out of it." Ruth slid off the examining table and stood to her feet, boring her gaze into Doctor Luke's. "The decision to seek treatment, or *not*, will always be mine."

"I'm not happy about it, but you're right, Ruth. Life is all about choices, and everybody has the right to make their own. Even when it comes to their health. But with every choice, comes a repercussion—some for the better, some for the worse."

Ruth nodded. "Exactly."

"Speaking of repercussions, I'll add this last reminder." Doctor Luke furrowed his brows. "We should remember our past mistakes and learn from them, but you haven't. When you started getting sick, you ignored the signs and symptoms. And when you finally came to get a checkup, the disease had spread to other parts of your body. Which is why we couldn't do surgery—the cancer had progressed to its final stage."

Ruth's lips quivered and tears streamed down her face. She couldn't argue with Doctor Luke, for she could only blame herself for waiting too long to see a doctor. Lydia walked over to her mother and wrapped her arms around her, speaking words of encouragement over her as the tears continued to flow down Ruth's face. Doctor Luke frowned as remorse gripped his heart. He wished he hadn't been so hard on Ruth, but at the same time, he wanted to keep her from making another wrong decision pertaining to her health.

"Ruth, I'm very sorry to have upset you, but discontinuing your medications really concerns me." He turned to the computer. "Despite not taking them for the past few days, your vital signs look excellent. And if you'd like a second opinion about continuing your medications, I'll notify Doctor Aaron. But for now, let's get you ready for a physical examination."

Ruth wiped the tears from her eyes, Lydia still at her side. "Sounds good."

"Your daughter is welcome to stay in the room if you'd like," said Doctor Luke.

Ruth looked at Lydia. "It's fine with me, so it's up to you."

Lydia nodded and then she took a seat as Doctor Luke handed her mother a gown to dress in. He then left the room to give Ruth some privacy, including Lydia who turned her head in the opposite direction. Lydia used this time to silently pray on her mother's behalf.

Once the examination was over, Doctor Luke left the room again so Ruth could get dressed. A couple minutes later, he walked back in with a sense of ease about him, which caused Ruth and Lydia to finally relax. They spoke for a little while longer, and before Ruth and Lydia left, he told Ruth to come back for another checkup on Wednesday, and she agreed.

On the day of Ruth's appointment, Lydia woke up early in the morning and praised God for her mother's well-being. It had been a week, and Ruth was still feeling as good as ever. Lydia then closed her eyes and prayed, asking for another favorable outcome of Doctor Luke's report.

After eating breakfast and getting ready, Ruth and Lydia headed to the doctor's office. When they arrived, the friendly receptionist told them to take a seat, reassuring them that their wait wouldn't be long. Lydia flipped through a magazine as Ruth strove with her thoughts. She wondered if a miracle was happening, or if some kind of unexpected scientific incident was taking place in her body.

"Ms. Mahlon?" The sweet voice shook Ruth out of her thoughts.

"Yes," responded Ruth.

The nurse smiled. "We're ready to see you."

"Ok." Ruth returned the smile as she and Lydia got up.

They followed the nurse to the same room where Ruth had her first examination a couple days ago. Lydia took a seat on the beige leather armchair as her mother perched herself on top of the examining table.

"My name's Eden, and I'll be checking your vitals today."

Eden wrapped the blood pressure cuff around Ruth's arm.

"How are you feeling, Ruth?"

"I'm doing great, praise God."

Eden's face lit up. "And you look great too."

"Thank you."

"So, is this your daughter?"

"Yes, this is Lydia."

"Hi, honey, nice to meet you."

"You too," replied Lydia.

Eden checked the rest of Ruth's vitals and then recorded them on the computer. "Everything looks good, Ruth. So what brings you back today?"

"To talk with Doctor Luke, regarding my previous visit." She took in a deep breath. "We're going to discuss my lab work along with the other test results."

"Anticipating results is always nerve-racking, but according to your blood pressure reading, you're handling it so well." Eden's mouth curled up into a genuine smile.

"Thank you, that makes me feel better."

"You're welcome." Eden turned back to the computer screen. "Oh, ok...I see when you came into the office this past Monday."

"Yep, I sure did," replied Ruth. "I wanted to be checked out because of the unexpected changes in my body, but for the better."

Ruth went into further detail about the positive changes in her health since she had stopped taking her medications. Lydia smiled and nodded the entire time, confirming her mother's report.

"Do you believe in miracles, Eden?"

"I sure do, honey. I've experienced them myself, and have seen them many times in my career."

"If you don't mind, can you pray for me?" asked Ruth.

"I'd love to, honey."

The three of them huddled in a small circle and joined hands. And when they closed their eyes and bowed their heads, Eden began to pray.

"Father God, thank you so much for this wonderful family. And thank you for giving them the courage to seek your face. I ask you to give them unwavering faith, trusting in you as the Healer, and to give them peace about the test results. Thank you, Father, for giving me this opportunity to mitigate their burdens and to encourage them. May your loving power and Spirit strengthen their heart. In Jesus's name. Amen!"

"Amen!" repeated Ruth and Lydia.

"Thank you so much, Eden, for your powerful prayer," said Ruth.

"It's my pleasure, honey." Eden hugged Ruth and Lydia before leaving the examining room, but when she reached the door, she turned back around. "And Ruth, keep up the faith."

Ruth smiled. "I will." She respected Doctor Luke, and appreciated all he had done for her, but her trust in God for a miracle was greater than the treatments and medications she had received.

Shortly after Eden had left, Doctor Luke entered the room. "Well hello there, ladies. How are the both of you doing?"

"I'm still feeling better than ever," replied Ruth. "How are you?"

Doctor Luke smiled. "Likewise, thanks for asking. So, any changes since Monday?"

"No. But I have been taking my medications—just not the same way I used to."

"What do you mean?" Doctor Luke tensed his jaw.

"Meaning, I've been taking them once a day rather than three times a day. I don't feel the need to take so many doses." Ruth gulped. "Honestly, I don't feel the need to take my medications at all."

Heat rose to Doctor Luke's face, his jaw tensing even more. His tangible frustration caused Ruth's heart to beat rapidly. She pressed her lips in a firm line as she rubbed her sweaty palms together. Lydia sank in her chair, wishing she could disappear.

He pulled up her records on the computer and eased up a little. "Well, your blood pressure, heart rate, temperature, and oxygen saturation looks great."

Ruth noticed the tension leaving Doctor Luke, so she relaxed her shoulders and blew out a breath of solace.

"After I get your test results, we'll talk more about your medications." Doctor Luke forced a smile and then walked out of the examining room.

"Ok," replied Ruth in a small voice.

Ruth and Lydia exchanged worried looks, but before they could express their concerns, Doctor Luke walked back into the room. They eyeballed the test results in his hands.

"This morning, I spoke with your oncologist, Doctor Aaron, regarding the test results."

"Ok," replied Ruth flatly.

"I'm going to order a second test for you, at a different facility." Doctor Luke crossed his arms over his chest, the test results still in his grip. "And I want you to take it as soon as possible."

A *thump* echoed in the room as the soles of Ruth's shoes hit the floor. Her brows bunched together, her forehead wrinkled. "Why's that?"

"Because we don't want to take any chances with your health. A week of you feeling good—isn't enough to convince me, or Doctor Aaron, concerning the remission of your cancer. We want to make sure that your test results from today, matches up with the next one...before we make any conclusions."

"I understand," began Ruth, "but you still haven't told me the results."

"As I said before, all your vital signs look great. And concerning the ultrasound, your complete blood count, and all of your blood work, they look great as well. However, the results are showing something unusual, which is another reason why Doctor Aaron and I want you to repeat the test."

Ruth and Lydia nodded their understanding.

"Now onto your medications," said Doctor Luke. "We will not endorse you to stop taking them, but we will taper your dosages based on your agreeable test results. Do you have any questions?"

No. But I wished you believed in miracles, thought Ruth.

With a heavy heart Ruth asked, "When's my next appointment?"

CHAPTER 15

It had been a week since Ruth and Lydia visited the facility Doctor Luke had assigned her to visit. They performed more urine and blood samples along with an MRI and CT scan. And today was the day when Ruth would receive the final verdict of her condition. Either a miracle was taking place in her body, or the medications she had taken—before discontinuing them—had cured her somehow.

Ruth and Lydia walked into familiar territory, feeling as if they were visiting relatives, or close friends. In the past two weeks, they have spent more time inside waiting and examining rooms than any other place. Everything came as second nature: the stack of magazines that were worth going through and the best water fountain to drink out of. But it was worth it because the staff members were always friendly and encouraging. Especially Eden—the nurse who always brightened Ruth's and Lydia's visits.

This time, Eden had led them to a different examining room. She took Ruth's vitals and then she left to get Doctor Luke. Ruth and Lydia sat in silence, hoping that today would be distinct, for the better.

Ruth and Lydia raised their heads when they heard a soft tap on the door. It was Doctor Luke. He walked into the room, holding several pieces of stapled paper. A shaft of hope seemed to illuminate the room as he broke the silent tension with a cheerful greeting and smile.

They gawked as Doctor Luke sat on the gray leather stool, pulling up her vitals on the computer screen, including a bunch of diagnostic images. He swiveled around and noticed the intrigue sparkling in their eyes, the worried lines embedded on their foreheads.

"Ruth, before we discuss your final test results"—he sat up straighter—"have you been doing anything different during the course of your treatment? Like taking dietary supplements, or changing your diet?"

"No, I haven't."

"Interesting...so you started feeling better a couple weeks ago, when you stopped taking your medications." His comment was more of a summary than a question.

"Correct. But I did start taking my medications again after you and Doctor Aaron insisted that I did."

"And we are so glad that you followed doctors' orders." He chuckled as he used air quotes.

This made Ruth and Lydia laugh as well.

"My daughter and I were chatting during lunch time, and she had mentioned not seeing me take my medication before we ate. Then, she pointed out the bread full of gluten I had ate as well!" Ruth looked over at Lydia who nodded her head in agreement. "And that's when I realized I wasn't feeling sick."

Doctor Luke unfolded his arms. "Well, I have your final test results from Mercy Institute of Health."

Ruth's eyes rounded as her body tensed and tingled with anticipation.

"Just so you know, I *do* believe in miracles," said Doctor Luke. "But I've only witnessed one during the twenty-five years of my career. And now, I can say I have witnessed two—there are no more indications of the disease in your body. You are cancer-free, Ruth."

Ruth almost fell off the examining table as Lydia clenched the sides of the armchair. Doctor Luke beamed as he stood up and handed Ruth the stack of papers that proved she was healed. Lydia eyed the exchange as she remained glued to the chair. He pointed at the medical terms and explained what they meant. He then walked over to the computer and pointed at the imaging results, explaining to her what they meant as well.

"Ruth, your days of having blood drawn, taking scans...have come to an end. But as for your medications, Doctor Aaron and I need you to take them for another week, or a little more, to avoid any relapses. Other than that, your chemo and other treatments are officially over." Doctor Luke beamed.

Ruth and Lydia jumped to their feet and lunged toward each other. They squealed as they held each other tight, tears of gladness running down their faces as they praised God for performing a miracle in Ruth's body.

"Ruth, as I told you before, you're my second patient to experience a miracle. The first one I witnessed happened to a man, who is still under my primary care. To this day, he is living life to the fullest, free from the terminal illness that once plagued him years ago. And just like you, he believed the healing hands of Jesus is what restored him to total health. You both share remarkable stories of survival against all odds, which increases my faith in the ultimate Healer."

So he does believe in miracles, thought Ruth. A huge smile followed.

Ruth flung her arms around Doctor Luke, telling him how grateful she was to have such a wonderful doctor and medical team. For they had done their best in treating her while she was sick.

After Ruth and Lydia left the doctors office, they were eager to share the glorious news with the person who had been there for them since day one—Pastor Paul. Ruth was overwhelmed with joy and gladness, thanking the Lord in her heart for hearing their prayers, and for blessing her with a loving daughter whose faith paved the way to her healing.

Their excitement intensified as they approached the gate, and once they entered the church grounds, Ruth and Lydia picked up their pace, oblivious to the squirrels scampering about.

One of the deacons greeted them as they walked through the front entrance, and then gestured for them to take a seat. They slid into one of the pews and when the deacon turned to leave, Ruth had stopped him. She asked if he could get Pastor Paul before service began, telling him it was urgent. He nodded his agreement to find him, and then like a couple of little girls, they giggled and fidgeted in their seats as they waited for Pastor Paul.

After what seemed like an eternity, the deacon walked out from the lobby with Pastor Paul at his side. They made their way to the front entrance of the church, and when the deacon pointed to the last pew, Pastor Paul's eyes widened. He did not expect to see Ruth and Lydia sitting there.

"What a lovely surprise to see the both of you here!" Pastor Paul beamed. "Thank you so much for visiting."

He extended his arm for a handshake, grateful but yet curious as to what brought Ruth and Lydia to church.

"How have the both of you been?" asked Pastor Paul.

"I'm doing great, thank you." Ruth's countenance glowed with joy. "How about you?"

"Good—really good. All glory to the Lord." Pastor Paul's eyes gleamed with delight.

Lydia smiled. "I bet you didn't expect to see us here, right?"

A slight blush rose to his cheeks. "No, I didn't. But I couldn't be happier."

"Ditto." Ruth smiled.

"Ruth, has your health been improving?" asked Pastor Paul. "Because you look absolutely fantastic."

"Actually, it has"—Ruth inhaled a breath—"which is why we're here."

Pastor Paul knitted his brows. "Ok..."

"I've had more doctor appointments in the past couple weeks than I've ever had. And this morning, I had another check up."

"Uh-huh." Pastor Paul shifted his weight, his arms crossing over his chest.

"After numerous blood tests and scans"—Ruth stood to her feet—"Doctor Luke told me I'm cancer-free."

Lydia jumped to her feet and took her mother's hand in hers. They smiled up at Pastor Paul as streams of joy ran down their faces.

"And we wanted you to know," said Ruth.

Pastor Paul's mouth fell open. "What?"

Lydia giggled. "It's true, Pastor Paul. My mom received her healing. It's a—"

"Miracle." Pastor Paul took a step forward and wrapped Ruth and Lydia in his arms. "Oh, my Lord! Blessed be His name." Tears gushed from his eyes. "Thank you Father God, and thank you Lord Jesus, for taking Ruth's sickness away. And thank you for making her whole."

Pulling away from their embrace, Pastor Paul took their hands into his, and then raised them toward the heavenlies.

"This is the day that the Lord has made, so we will rejoice and be exceedingly glad in it!" Without knowing what was going on, the entire congregation stood up and rejoiced with Pastor Paul, Ruth and Lydia. But then, everyone started asking questions, wanting to know why they were praising the Lord.

Pastor Paul switched his gaze back to Ruth and Lydia, holding a finger to his lips. They nodded their heads, understanding his gesture of keeping quiet. He then addressed the others, promising to share the wonderful news with them, but not until after service would begin. With eager expressions, they sat back down, talking with one another as to what the news could be about.

"Ruth, I would love for you to share what the Lord has done for you," began Pastor Paul. "It would bless the church so much more if it came from your lips instead of mine. What do you say?"

Ruth's heart skipped a beat as her hands twitched. "The thought of speaking to a room full of people makes me nervous. But, how can I *not* share with them what the Lord has done for me?"

"And I'll be there with you, right at your side," said Pastor Paul. "You have nothing to fear, Ruth. For your testimony will greatly encourage the congregation."

"Thank you so much, Pastor Paul, for everything." Ruth teared up again.

"You're welcome, but I'm not the only one to thank." Pastor Paul looked over at Lydia. "You have an amazing child who loves you so much. And her prayers were heard, even before mine."

"They sure were." Ruth pulled Lydia in for another hug. "I have the best support team ever."

CHAPTER 16

Pastor Paul glanced down at his watch—service would be starting shortly. He parted ways with Ruth and Lydia and then made his way to the front entrance, cutting a left toward the lobby where the restrooms were located. When he traced his steps back to the front entrance, he noticed more people filing in through the front doors. He welcomed all of them, including a young girl.

"Well, hello there, young lady." Pastor Paul held up his hand, giving her a high-five. "Glad you could make it for today's service."

The girl smiled. "Thanks, Pastor Paul, me too."

"Tonight is going to be very special...Remember the young girl I told you about? The one who accepted Jesus as her personal Savior not long ago."

"Yeah." The girl nodded.

"Well, she's here...with her mother."

The girl beamed. "That's awesome!"

"Indeed it is. And I'll make sure to introduce her to you after service. I believe the both of you will become very good friends. She needs someone to guide her with her new life in the Lord—and I believe you're the person to do just that."

He placed a gentle hand on her back.

"Go ahead and find a seat before they're all taken." With that, Pastor Paul walked away and disappeared through a door—opposite of the lobby—located at the front of the church.

The young girl searched the overflowing pews, thinking she would have to stand at the back of the church for the entire service. But then a few of her friends from youth group spotted her and waved her over to sit with them.

A few more people trickled in, searching for a place to sit, as Ruth and Lydia looked at each other in confusion. Those around them mumbled words and sounds they couldn't comprehend. They assumed they were praying due to their bowed heads. Still, Ruth and Lydia sidled up to each other, feeling very uncomfortable and out of place.

The worship leader walked onto the stage and the congregation grew quiet. He greeted them and then made his cue for everyone to stand up. Ruth and Lydia swayed back and forth to the melodious music, the sound of lovely voices and lyrics uplifting their souls.

After singing a few songs, the worship leader walked off the stage as Pastor Paul made his way to the podium. He welcomed all the members of the church, including the visitors. The congregation responded back with a round of applause along with several "amens."

"Before we get into the Word of God and the message He has for us today, please stand up and join me in prayer. Dear Heavenly Father...."

Pastor Paul ended the prayer and asked everyone to be seated once again.

"I know everyone is excited for today's message, but please bear with me just a little longer." Pastor Paul's gaze swept over the pews at the front of the church, a smile spreading across his face when he spotted Ruth and Lydia. "Church, there are two very special visitors among us today, and I'd like for you to give them a warm welcome."

Excited murmurs erupted as curious faces searched around for the special guests.

"Ruth and Lydia, please come up here and join me," said Pastor Paul.

With weak knees, clammy hands, and rapid heart beats, Ruth and Lydia stood to their feet. Pastor Paul beamed as he and the rest of the congregation applauded on their behalf. They blushed, responding with lopsided smiles as strange but friendly faces greeted them on their way to the stage. Pastor Paul met them at the steps and then escorted them to the podium.

"The Lord has greatly impacted the lives of this mother and daughter, standing before you, in a short amount of time," began Pastor Paul. "And their testimonies will encourage you, increasing your faith in profound ways."

A huge lump formed in Ruth's throat, so she swallowed several times, trying to get rid of it. Lydia clamped her hands together, hoping to stop the trembling.

"A few weeks ago, this young lady"—Pastor Paul gestured toward Lydia—"stopped by our church, seeking prayer for her mother. And after several conversations, endless prayer, and a couple of home visitations, Lydia opened the door of her heart to the Lord—she is now a fellow sister in Christ."

Joyous clasps and shouts erupted from the congregation.

"But there's more," continued Pastor Paul. "Because of Lydia's determination, persistence and courage, the Lord has intervened in her mother's life as well. I have had the opportunity to converse and pray for the both of them along with Pastor Jonathan and Grace, our church secretary." He reached for Ruth's hand and she placed it in his. "I'm so grateful for Ruth inviting us into her home—and into her life."

He stepped back from the podium, and in a quiet voice, he asked Ruth if she was ready to share her testimony with the church. Despite how nervous she was, she nodded her head, hoping the Lord would give her the strength and peace she needed. She only knew a few people among the crowded sanctuary of strangers. Even at that, those she knew were only on a basic level. Regret and guilt started to attack her, but she refused to focus on her life of isolation, pain, and bitterness. So instead, she inhaled a deep breath and stepped up to the podium.

"Hi, my name is Ruth. And I'm glad to be here."

She started her journey from the beginning—when Lydia had tried out for the singing contest. And how she had hoped to win so she could pay for her doctor bills, medications, and treatments. Then, she told them about Lydia's summer job, hoping it would get them by while searching for other means of support: both financial and emotional.

Lydia pulled her gaze away from the crowd, and stared down at her shoes, not able to endure their attention, although positive.

Ruth went on to talk about her illness, her weekly trips to the doctor's office, and all the tests she had to take. Sniffles, watery eyes, and whispers of compassion followed her account.

"Living with cancer seemed like an impossible journey, one I never thought I would see to the end. But because of my loving and amazing daughter, along with Pastor Paul and the others, I was able to make it through each day, finding glimpses of hope all around me."

Ruth reached a hand toward Lydia and gazed lovingly into her eyes. She took hold of her mother's hand, and then Ruth pulled her forward, right next to her.

"...And as hard as I tried to deny God's existence and His love for me, He still pursued me, waiting for me to let

Him into my heart," continued Ruth. "There are no words that can express how eternally grateful I am to be standing here in front of all of you." With the back of her hand, Ruth wiped away the tears from her face. "For anyone who has doubts about God, I'm here to testify that He is real. He is love. And He is powerful. Because of Him, I am cancer-free."

Praises and shouts of glee exploded as the congregation jumped to their feet. Ruth, Lydia, and Pastor Paul stood in total awe as they raised their hands and danced around while others spoke in tongues and knelt to the ground to pray.

"Thank you, Ruth, for sharing your miraculous testimony. The Lord has been so good and faithful to you and your daughter." Pastor Paul wrapped an arm around Ruth's shoulder and the other around Lydia's. "Just in case you are not aware, Ruth and Lydia live in the neighborhood, not too far from the church...And now, I'd like to pray for them, but I need more than one witness to do so. Does anyone happen to know this precious, little family?"

A raised hand made its appearance from the middle of the church. Pastor Paul tilted his head and squinted his eyes, trying to make out who it was.

"The person with the raised hand, can you please stand up so we can see you better?" asked Pastor Paul.

A teenage girl surrounded by other youths stood to her feet. Tears gushed down her face and then she began weeping. Lydia's eyes rounded in utter shock as she brought a hand up to her mouth. She couldn't believe it, but yet there was *no* denying who was standing in the middle of the church—it was Abigail. Her best friend.

Ruth was just as shocked. She turned to Lydia and pulled her in for a hug, asking if she was all right. For she knew how her daughter was feeling since Lydia and Abigail haven't spoken in quite some time. But all Lydia could do was cry in her mother's arms.

Compassion gripped Pastor's Paul heart. "Lydia, do you know Abigail?"

Lydia sniffled and nodded. "Yeah."

"I hope those are happy tears"—Pastor Paul placed a hand on Lydia's back—"because if they're not, I'm so sorry for causing you any—"

"You didn't cause any trouble," interrupted Ruth. "Abigail's her best friend."

Lydia lifter her head, tears glistening on her face. "She *was* my best friend."

Clarity, understanding and confirmation came to Pastor Paul's mind along with the conversations he and Lydia had about her friend—the girl standing in the middle pew with a tear-streaked face. The same girl they had been talking about all this time. He rubbed the back of his neck, not knowing what to do. He didn't want to cause Lydia more stress by having Abigail come up and pray for them. But he didn't want to leave Abigail standing in awkward suspense, making her feel as if her support was not wanted. That she wasn't wanted. Thankfully, the Holy Ghost laid it on his heart to invite Abigail up to the podium, so that the Lord could reconcile their friendship.

With compassionate eyes, Pastor Paul laid both hands on Lydia's shoulders. "Lydia, the Lord deeply cares about you and He wants to heal all your emotional wounds. He also wants to restore your friendship with Abigail...all you have to do is allow Him to."

Lydia nodded as a soft "ok" escaped her lips.

Taking a deep breath, Pastor Paul gestured toward Abigail. "Come up here, darling."

Abigail wiped the tears from her face with the back of her hand and then sidestepped her way out of the pew. Lydia tried to steady her breath as Abigail approached the stage. With an arm wrapped around Lydia, Ruth wrapped her other one around Abigail as she joined them next to the podium.

"Thank you, Father, for your everlasting goodness and faithfulness. And thank you for the miracles you have done in Ruth's and Lydia's lives." Pastor Paul turned to face Lydia and Abigail, grinning from ear to ear. "And for reuniting these very special young ladies."

The congregation joined in the celebration with shouts and praises as the girls exchanged sideways glances, giggling with teary eyes. Ruth pulled them in for a tight squeeze, thanking the Lord in her heart for all He had done.

The girls were huddled together, chatting away, so Pastor Paul looked over at Ruth. "Before you ladies take a seat, is there anything else you'd like to say?"

Ruth nodded. "I sure do."

Pastor Paul took a step back as Ruth stepped up to the podium once again.

"As living proof, be encouraged that God still performs miracles."

CHAPTER 17

Pastor Paul reached for a box of tissues sitting on a small table, next to the podium, and handed it to Ruth. She passed it on to the girls next. The congregation cheered once more as the three of them walked off the stage and down the aisle. Everyone in the pew, where Ruth and Lydia had sat, scooted down to make room for them, including Abigail.

Raising his hands above his head, Pastor Paul shouted, "What a remarkable and mighty God we serve!" He then proceeded with his sermon, which was followed by another round of worship songs and an alter call, where several people came forward, accepting Jesus as their personal Lord and Savior.

After the service had ended, everybody exchanged greetings while Abigail and Lydia remained seated in the pew, catching up on life during their time apart.

"I—I still can't believe it." Abigail stared at Lydia with wonderment. "This feels like a dream, you know?"

"It really does." Lydia smiled.

"I prayed, a lot, over the summer. And I cried every day, missing my best friend." Abigail took hold of Lydia's hand. "But tonight, my prayers were *finally* answered."

"Same." Lydia sniffled. "I talked a lot about you to Pastor Paul, and he told me about a girl who attended church with the same name. It's funny 'cause we weren't sure if we were talking about the same person or not."

Abigail propped an elbow on top of the pew and rested her chin on it.

"I should have know, though," continued Lydia. " I mean, how many girls in this small town fit your description?"

Abigail giggled. "True to that."

Ruth walked up to where the girls were sitting, smiling as big as they were. She was beyond happy to see them getting along after all this time. Today was a wonderful day for Ruth and Lydia. And for Abigail too.

With all the excitement, however, it had worn Ruth out. She was ready to go home. But Lydia wasn't.

"Mom, can I please stay a little longer? We still have lots to talk about."

"Of course, honey, take your time. But make sure to call me before you head home, ok?"

"I will, don't worry." Lydia stood up to give her mother a hug. "See ya later. Love you."

"Love you too."

Abigail was still sitting, so Ruth bent over to give her a hug before she left.

"Just so you know, Lydia wasn't the only one who missed you. I did too," said Ruth.

Abigail was touched beyond words by Ruth's statement. She squeezed Ruth with all of her heart, feeling grateful to be reconnected with Lydia and her mother. Ruth said her goodbyes and then she turned to leave. But on her way toward the front entrance, a myriad of delighted faces surrounded her. The members of the church expressed how encouraged they were by her testimony, and many of them gave her their contact information, wanting to stay connected.

After more hugging and praying, Ruth walked out of the church, and smiled up at the sky, feeling abundantly blessed. Besides being cured of her terminal sickness, she beamed at the sense of finally belonging. For Ruth would not have to do life alone anymore.

"Oh my goodness, Lydia, I can't thank the Lord enough for your mom's healing," said Abigail.

"Me too," replied Lydia. "Everything we went through was worth it. He took my striving of wanting to help my mom, and took over, blessing us more than imaginable."

"Amen!"

"He also used my mom's sickness as a means of my salvation, including hers."

"As the saying goes, 'When it rains, it pours.'" Abigail lifted her face toward the ceiling. "God opened the floodgates of Heaven, showering you and your mom with miracles, including the restoration of our friendship."

Lydia leaned in to give Abigail a hug. "I prayed, just like you did—and here we are."

"Yep. Here we are." Abigail beamed. "The Lord arranged everything in a way nobody thought would happen."

"It's so true." Lydia stood up and extended a hand toward Abigail. "Wanna go outside and finish chatting? There's only a few people left in here, besides us."

Abigail looked around. "Wow. You're right."

They debated where to go to hang out, and then decided on a place that wasn't too far from the church, or from Lydia's house. They walked a little ways down the sidewalk and crossed the street, where the bus stop was at. Lydia sat on one end of the bench as Abigail sat on the other.

"I'm really sorry for all the mean things I've said," began Lydia. "And for ignoring you."

"You don't have to be sorry, Lydia. You were under a lot of stress, and no one was there to help you and your mom. If anyone should be apologizing, it should be me. I should have been there for you, but instead, all I did was guilt-trip you the entire time."

"It's ok. You meant well, like you always do." Lydia stared out in the distance. "Plus, my stubbornness didn't help. You had every right to get frustrated with me."

"Yeah, you can be pretty stubborn."

The girls laughed.

"Anyways, I believe this was God's appointed time for everything. Your mom's healing, and how the both of you gave your lives to Christ, is what matters the most. Bitterness, unforgiveness, regret, fear, negative emotions, including negative mindsets, have no value in this life. Or in the life to come. The only thing they do is steal our joy, swaying us to give up fighting the good fight of faith...."

"You're right. You always are. I can't thank you enough for your relentless prayers. My mom and I are super blessed to have you in our lives." Lydia turned to look at Abigail. "Thanks for not giving up on me."

Abigail sighed. "To be honest, I almost did. But I thank God for giving me strength and patience. The Bible says, 'Call to me and I'll answer you, and show you great and mighty things which you do not know.'"

"You're so blessed when it comes to memorizing the Word of God. And hopefully, I'll be able to do the same some day. I even told Pastor Paul how equipped you are with bringing up relevant Scriptures at the right time."

Abigail's eyes lit up with gladness. "Thanks. But all of God's children, which includes you, have the same ability to speak the right Scriptures over our circumstances, including the circumstances of others. You just have to study and pray for the Lord to help you."

Lydia nodded, looking encouraged.

"The Bible talks about how to defend ourselves from the enemy," continued Abigail. "And we do so by putting on the spiritual armor of God."

"The armor of God? How did I not know about this? Anyways, that sounds super cool! Can you teach me more about it, including how to memorize Bible verses?"

Abigail smiled. "I'd be honored to."

Lydia listened intently as Abigail explained the basics of spiritual warfare along with how to use the armor of God to defend oneself from the enemy. She also gave her tips on how to recall certain Scriptures when needed. Lydia was fascinated by the spiritual realm and how it correlated with the mundane.

"I just realized I haven't asked about your mom," said Lydia. "I've been so focused catching up with you that I forgot. I'm so sorry."

Abigail's expression fell flat. "It's ok."

"Are you sure? You look kinda upset. But you have every right to be."

Abigail hunched over and stared at the ground.

"I wasn't the only one with a sick mom—how's she's doing?" asked Lydia.

Abigail remained silent.

"Abigail, what's wrong?"

All of a sudden, Lydia was overcome with guilt. Her summer had been consumed with working a part-time job, taking care of her mother, visiting doctors' offices, and being mad at Abigail. She felt unworthy to have such an amazing friend—a friend who had always been there for her, and for her mother. Lydia kept apologizing until Abigail asked her to stop.

"I'm not mad at you, Lydia. I'm just—"Abigail brought her hands up to her face and began to cry.

Lydia placed a gentle hand on Abigail's back. "I'm guessing she's not doing so good since she wasn't with you at church, right?"

"We'll talk about it later, ok?" Abigail lifted her head up and stared straight ahead. "Besides, it's getting dark. We should leave before your mom gets worried."

"I don't care," started Lydia. "I'll sit here and listen as long as you need me to."

"Thanks. But I really don't want to talk about it right now."

"Despite shutting each other out over the summer, I never stopped caring about you. You're my best friend, and you always will be." Lydia wiped away at the tear cascading down her cheek. "Just tell me what's going on."

"My—my mom. She's—"Abigail struggled for words. "She's gone."

Lydia arched a brow. "Gone? Like away at a hospital?"

Abigail shook her head.

"Like she's visiting relatives?"

Again, Abigail shook her head.

"Is she on vacation?" Lydia's heart raced as Abigail gushed tears. "You're scaring me, Abby. Where's your mom?"

"She's gone—she went to be with the Lord."

Lydia's breath caught. Time seemed to stand still as she gaped at Abigail. Life had never been easy for Lydia and her mother, and even though Ruth could have died, the Lord healed her. But why did He not come through for Abigail's mother? After all, she and Abigail were believers too. Not only had they been walking longer, but they were stronger, more mature, and more devoted than Lydia and her mother were.

Every fiber of Abigail's being felt weightless—her life all of a sudden seeming surreal. Up until this point, the

Holy Ghost had given her supernatural strength, peace and comfort to except the death of her mother. But now, it seemed as if His protective shield over her soul had been removed, bearing the raw feelings of losing a loved one.

After a couple minutes of the girls sitting in utter shock, Abigail somehow managed to scoot closer to Lydia. Without even thinking, she draped an arm around Lydia and rested her head on her shoulder.

"It's ok, Lydia." Abigail shuddered as chills ran through her body. "She's in a much better place now."

"I'm the most selfish person that ever lived on this earth." Lydia cringed and gritted her teeth as mental accusations tormented her:

You're the worst friend ever. You don't deserve any blessings.

"You needed me just as much as I needed you," continued Lydia. "But my mom's sickness blinded me to the fact that your mom was sick too." She locked her watery gaze into Abigail's. "I don't know what to say, except that I'm so sorry. I'm so, so, sorry she's gone."

Abigail tightened her grip around Lydia. "It's no one's fault my mom got sick. And by no means is it anyone's fault that she passed away. It was just her time to go."

Taking a moment to settle her emotions, Abigail closed her eyes and asked the Holy Ghost to release His comfort, to wrap them up in His magnificent peace.

"Lydia, I know it's hard to accept that she's not here anymore. But we should be rejoicing because there's no one else who could love her, and who can take care of her, the way the Lord can. Besides, we should also be rejoicing over your mom. It's a miracle, Lydia, that she's alive and cancer-free."

"I love you, Abby. And I'm so grateful that the Lord has brought you into my life." Lydia placed an arm around Abigail. "You're the best friend ever."

"And so are you." Abigail lifted her head off of Lydia's shoulder and scooted back, just a little, to look her in the eyes. "I hope those are happy tears."

Lydia giggled. "You're the second person to say that."

She told Abigail when Pastor Paul had made that same comment to her when she and her mother were standing with him on stage, hoping she was crying out of joy when saw Abigail stand up during service.

"Abby, when did your mom...?"

"Almost three weeks ago."

Lydia stood up to stretch and then crossed her arms over her chest. "I still can't believe you didn't say anything about your mom getting worse, even though we weren't talking. I would have pushed our differences aside, supporting the both of you during that time. I mean it, Abby."

"I know you do, but I didn't want to be a setback in your life." Abigail stood to her feet as well. "And I didn't want to destroy the faith that I was trying to build up in you. I also told you about Jesus being our Healer, and I didn't want to discourage you by talking about how sick my mom was—you barely had any hope for your own mom at the time. So I didn't want to hinder your faith and trust in the Lord...I hope you understand."

Lydia was speechless. She was beyond humbled, and in total awe, by Abigail's faith, strength...and selflessness. For Abigail had been more concerned about Lydia's faith than stressing her out about her own mother's terminal sickness. Lydia was so inspired by her best friend's maturity in the Lord, but doubted she could be as deeply rooted as Abigail was. She struggled with what she would do if she were in Abigail's shoes, trying to be a light and encouragement to someone else while enduring hardships of her own.

Abigail reached for Lydia's hands and held them gently in hers. "Focus on the blessings you've received:

your mom's healing and her salvation. *Your* salvation."
Abigail's face had a heavenly glow to it. "My mom died as
a believer. And she'll live with the Lord forever along with
all of His children. This includes us, too, Lydia."

Self-conviction and remorse loosened its grip around
Lydia's soul.

"Thank you for expelling the lies in my heart, and in
my head, with God's Word," said Lydia. "There's a
Scripture that helped me get through the days during my
mom's sickness. It's the one that talks about God not
giving us more than we can handle."

"Preach it, sister!" Abigail's smile reached her eyes.

Joyous laughter followed as the girls threw their
heads back, smiling up at the stars.

"It's getting pretty dark," said Lydia. "You wanna stay
the night at my house?"

Abigail smiled. "I'd love to."

The girls linked their arms and walked off into the
twilight. They continued to chat on their way to Lydia's
house, keeping in step with each other, but they still had
so much more to discuss, including how to break the
news to Ruth about Abigail's mother.

CHAPTER 18

On the way to the kitchen for another cup of coffee, Ruth stopped and turned around when the front door creaked open. Lydia and Abigail stood in the living room, their arms still linked. Ruth walked as fast as she could and then greeted them with a tight squeeze. And just like Lydia, Ruth wanted to catch up on Abigail's life, so she invited them to join her in the kitchen.

The girls sat down at the table as Ruth prepared something for them to snack on. Minutes later, she returned with a tray full of sandwiches and glasses that she placed in front of them. Ruth sat across from the girls and then she prayed. After thanking the Lord for their food, Lydia passed the tray around as Ruth filled their cups with water.

Ruth was brought up to speed on Abigail's life, but when she asked Abigail about her mother, a spiritual cloud of heaviness appeared over them. The awkward silence was too much to bear. She switched her gaze between the girls, wondering why they looked so grim. But then, the girls began to weep, and Ruth no longer needed an answer. It was evident that Abigail's mother had passed away.

Ruth walked around to the other side of the table where she wedged herself between the girls, embracing them as tight as she could. They wept and prayed until all their strength had withered away.

It was getting late, so the three of them headed upstairs. They stopped in front of Ruth's bedroom where she kissed them goodnight before heading to bed. After Ruth's door had closed behind her, the girls walked to the end of the hallway, making a right into the bathroom. Their energy was renewed after washing their faces and brushing their teeth. So by the time they had changed into comfy sweat pants and oversized T-shirts, they plopped onto Lydia's bed and chatted some more.

Fluffy pillows surrounded them as they sat crossed-legged from one another. Abigail grabbed a pillow and pressed it to her chest as they talked about Lydia's new life in Christ. But she wanted Lydia to go into further detail as to what inspired her to make that decision.

"...I was so hard-headed," said Lydia. "Especially about the Lord and religion."

Abigail rolled her eyes in mock gesture. "You can say that again."

"Not nice!" Lydia snatched up a pillow and tossed it at Abigail. "You didn't have to agree with me, you know?"

A war of pillows broke out soon after.

"Ok, ok. I surrender." Lydia was out of breath from laughing so hard, but she continued when she had regained her breathing. "So right after you left the store, I started thinking about the Lord. A lot. And everything you had said to me up to that point."

"And that was the day I thought we would never be friends again," admitted Abigail. "I even questioned my salvation, wondering if I was being a good witness to you or not."

"Abby, you were never the one in question—I was. Believe me, ok?"

Abigail nodded.

"So after I got off work that day, I walked across the street to the bus stop. As I waited for my ride home, a homeless man approached me and asked for a quarter. I gave him what I had and then he left. But then he came right back."

Abigail squeezed her pillow, her eyes raised in suspense. "What happened next?"

"He gave me a pamphlet that had a bunch of Scriptures in it, and a story about the Sacrificed Lamb. So I thanked him, slid it in my pocket, and then he left. But this time I watched him leave. He crossed the street and greeted a man who sat outside the grocery store."

"Oh, you're talking about Shalom," stated Abigail.

Lydia nodded. "Yep. The one and only. Anyways, the other man looked homeless too. And the man who had approached me, walked into the store and came back out with a small paper bag. He handed it to the other man whose face lit up. I couldn't hear what they were saying, but they seemed really happy."

"Hopefully it was food and not something like alcohol or cigarettes."

"Rest assured—it was food."

Abigail arched a brow. "Wait. How do you know that?"

"'Cause I went across the street to talk to them."

Lydia went on to tell Abigail how she had went into Shalom to purchase something to eat for the two men. She also told Abigail her reasoning as to why she did this. Abigail had a look of admiration when she heard of the homeless man's compassion for his friend. Even though they were both in need. Then, Lydia told her how she had missed the bus, but decided it was more important to stay and bless the men than to make it home on time.

"...their gratitude turned my heart into mush," said Lydia. "I never thought a couple of sandwiches could make someone so happy. Make that two people so happy!"

Abigail's eyes twinkled with delight. "Aw!"

"After that, we introduced ourselves, and then we got into a long conversation. Well technically, they did most of the talking. I just listened and asked lots of questions."

"So what's their names?"

"The man I gave the dollar to, is Daniel. And his friend's name is Joshua. Before I continue, though, I need to stretch. My back is killing me."

"So is mine. I've been hunched over the entire time."

The girls got up and stretched, and then they tiptoed down the stairs to get something to drink. When they returned to Lydia's room, they set their glasses on the nightstand and then lay across the bed, on their stomachs, their feet dangling off the other end.

"Daniel shared his life testimony, which was super inspiring," continued Lydia. "Come to find out, he had lung cancer...Hearing him speak gave me so much hope for mom to be healed too. But at first, I downplayed what he was saying, thinking he wasn't as sick as he had claimed to be. I couldn't believe anyone could ever be as sick as my mom was"—Lydia's throat tightened and her eyes welled up—"I'm so sorry, Abby. But I thought the same thing about your mom."

Abigail draped an arm over Lydia's back. "I've already forgiven you. But you need to forgive yourself."

"I've tried to but it's so hard. Will you pray for me?"

"Of course I will."

Abigail prayed and asked the Lord to help Lydia overcome any remorse and regret that held her captive. She also asked for the Holy Ghost to give her peace and patience as the Lord worked in her heart. Lydia felt much better and resumed her conversation with Abigail.

"Daniel was in his last stage of lung cancer and the doctors told him he only had a few months to live. But he kept the faith and asked his friend Joshua to pray for him. And soon after he did, Daniel was healed—just like that."

"Just like that?"

Lydia nodded. "Just like that. Anyways, we talked a little longer while I waited for the next bus to arrive. I even asked them to pray for my mom. And you know I've never asked for prayer before, not even from you."

"Tell me something I don't know." Abigail rolled her eyes again, making Lydia laugh. "But seriously, I'm so proud of you. I know that was a hard thing for you to do."

"It really was." Lydia exhaled. "One minute I was hopeful, and the next I doubted everything."

"Either way, it's obvious that hope had prevailed." Abigail smiled.

"It sure did." Lydia pushed herself up and sat back on her knees, resting her lower body on her heels. "We said our goodbyes and then I walked back to the bus stop. As I sat on the bench, the words Joshua had said to me echoed in my mind: 'He will make a way where there seems to be no way.' It resonated with me 'cause I really had nowhere to go at the time."

Abigail sat back on the bed as well. "Maybe the Lord wanted you to know about the free gift of His grace, a gift no one can earn—just like salvation."

"Exactly. I feel like the Lord wanted me to learn something from these men." Lydia paused, trying to recall something. "Oh, there was something else Joshua had said that sounded just like you."

"Really? What was it?"

"He said he was able to move forward by the grace of God. And now that I think about it, I know how you're able to get through every day without your mom. Only God can give someone the supernatural will and strength to carry on. No matter what."

"Amen to that!" Abigail raised her hands above her head, pumping them upwards toward the ceiling. "As a Christian, there's nothing more rewarding than seeing your prayers answered."

"Agreed." Lydia beamed. "But yeah, that's how my life with the Lord had started. You know what's weird, though? I haven't seen those men ever since that day. It's like they left town. Or disappeared."

"Or maybe they didn't."

"So what...they're hiding from me?"

Abigail grinned, her countenance glowing. "Do you believe in angels?"

CHAPTER 19

Not long after giving their testimonies, Ruth and Lydia started going to church on a regular basis. Lydia had also joined different youth programs, which made Abigail very happy. Pastor Paul was beyond grateful to see how quickly they had adjusted to their new lives in Christ.

After discipleship class, Ruth and Lydia prepared for their big day at church—they were going to be baptized. They used one of the Bible study rooms to change into clothes that would be appropriate for the special occasion.

Someone knocked on the door and Lydia answered it. Abigail and a small group of smiling women stood in the hallway. They were so eager and excited to prepare them for their baptisms. Huddling in the center of the room,

Abigail and the women gave thanks to the Lord for their salvation, and then they prayed over Ruth and Lydia.

The time had come, so Ruth's and Lydia's entourage of faith-filled women escorted them to the sanctuary.

Abigail was struggling with negative emotions, feeling bad for discouraging Lydia over her vocal talent. Even more so for making her feel guilty about trying out for the singing contest. She should have looked at Lydia's heart (her intentions) rather than getting carried away with her spiritual standards and advice that came off as legalistic.

So, it was time for Abigail to make things right. She had talked to the worship leader at church, recommending Lydia to try out for the choir. Lydia had such an exquisite voice and Abigail knew she was meant to share it with others. But when she had approached her about this, Lydia coward away from the idea. Thoughts of the singing contest resurfaced, creating stress and guilt Lydia didn't want to deal with. Most importantly, she didn't want to jeopardize her friendship with Abigail.

However, Lydia's reluctancy did not stop Abigail from pursuing her on this matter.

After much thought and prayer, Lydia had auditioned for the worship leader. And since Abigail had learned from the past, she delicately told Lydia to guard her heart, not allowing others to place their expectations, or negative opinions, on her concerning her talent. She also reminded Lydia of a Scripture from the book of Colossians where it talks about doing everything unto the Lord with your whole heart, and not for anyone else. Abigail was relieved and very happy when Lydia had received her advice with peace and motivation.

The Lord had finally worked everything out for Lydia's good. For He had secured a place for her within the church choir.

Abigail had spent the night at Lydia's house. And when the sun's rays peeked through the blinds, the girls regretted staying up too late. Yawning and stretching, they got out of bed and began to get ready for Sunday morning service.

Cheerful faces greeted Ruth and the girls as they walked inside the church. And as soon as they entered the lobby, Ruth was whisked away by a group of women—her new friends. They headed down the hallway, carrying on like a bunch of school girls. Lydia and Abigail looked at each other and giggled. Ruth's life was drastically changing for the better, and Lydia no longer worried about her mother's mental and emotional well-being.

Sunday classes were canceled, so the girls remained in the lobby. They plopped down on one of the couches as joyous laughter floated down the hallway—Ruth and her friends were having such a good time.

"Remember you told me about your Geometry class, and how you struggled with it last semester?" asked Abigail.

"How can I forget. I'm so gonna pay for it big time this coming up year." Lydia blew out an irritated breath." I should have listened to you."

"You can't go back in time, but you can move forward," began Abigail. "You're such a hard-working person, and I have no doubt you'll make it up this year."

"Thanks for the boost of confidence, Abby."

Abigail smiled. "You're welcome."

"And I promise to consider all you have to say from now on. I've reaped the consequences when I didn't listen to you in the past, and I don't wanna go there again."

"Aw...thanks. But stop beating yourself up over it. One of the ways we learn, is by our mistakes. And somehow, some way, the Lord always makes something good come out of them."

"Another score for Abigail—the best and wisest friend ever."

"And score to the most passionate person ever. Along with being the best singer in town."

Lydia blushed. "Thanks."

"So remember what happened when I decided to register for basketball last semester?" asked Abigail.

"Another moment I can't forget." Lydia giggled.

"Gee thanks." Abigail smirked. "My point is, you gave me good advice as well, but I didn't take it. It was so embarrassing not to score a single shot during the semester. Everybody made fun of me, saying, 'The ball itself isn't impressed with your efforts. Hopefully today you'll aim toward the net.'"

Lydia clapped a hand over her mouth, trying to muffle her laughter. "Seriously, they said that?"

"Glad you think it's funny." Abigail shot Lydia a glare. "But yeah, they did."

"Come on, you know you wanna laugh." Lydia kept making silly faces at Abigail until she couldn't keep a straight face anymore. They threw their heads back, laughing hysterically. But they were silenced when one of the deacons walked past them, fuming with agitation. His face was bright red and his nostrils flared out. The girls forced solemn expressions as they apologized. But once he left, they snickered behind his back.

"I have to confess something," started Abigail.

Lydia pinched her brows together. "Ok..."

"Singing contest or not, you have what it takes to be a successful singer. To be all famous and stuff. But I'm so glad you've decided to use your gift for the Lord's glory, instead of using it to entertain and please the world." Abigail drew in a breath. "Hate to bring up the past, but that's what I was trying to say when you were wanting to try out for the singing contest. But I totally botched how it came out. Sorry for hurting you, Lydia."

"It's cool. Don't worry about it. The past is the past. So leave it there, ok?"

Abigail nodded with a smile. "Ok."

With a few minutes left to spare, the girls talked about the Lord's salvation, and how nothing—absolutely nothing—was ever worth refusing it, or giving up on it. Whatever the world had to offer, it would never be worth it.

"I gotta use the restroom, will you watch my bag?" asked Lydia.

"Sure. But hurry back. Service will be starting any minute."

"Gotcha."

Ruth and her friends were walking down the hallway when Lydia zoomed past them. They waved at her, but she ducked into the restroom, oblivious to their presence. Laughter followed as they entered the lobby. They greeted Abigail as they passed by, making their way to the front entrance.

Abigail smiled at them and then looked up at the wall clock. Time was running out. She stood up and started walking toward the restrooms when someone called out her name—it was Pastor Paul. He stood in the hallway, motioning to her to come over.

"Hey, Pastor Paul."

"Hello, my dear. Is Lydia here today?"

"Yeah. She's in the restroom."

"Ok, great. Could you please tell her to meet me in my office after service? I need to discuss something with her."

Abigail struggled to pry for more answers. "Sure, I'll let her know."

"Thank you so much."

The deacon who had told the girls to keep it down, came up to Pastor Paul, alerting him that it was almost time for service to begin. Abigail bit her lower lip and looked away, sensing the deacon was still slightly annoyed with her and Lydia.

"I have to go, Abby. But I'll see you again inside the sanctuary." Pastor Paul and the deacon turned around and walked away, slipping through a door that led to the stage and pulpit.

Curiosity had sidetracked Abigail, making her forget to check on Lydia. Thoughts rushed through her mind as to what news Pastor Paul needed to share with her best friend. But then she was shaken out of her reverie when a hand gripped the back of her shoulder. A snicker followed as Abigail gasped.

She whirled around and saw Lydia standing in front of her. Relieved but annoyed, Abigail told Lydia about Pastor Paul wanting to see her after service. They rushed

out of the hallway, through the lobby, and into the crowded sanctuary. They slid into the back pew just in time.

Service had ended and half of the members stayed behind to chat while the others filed out the double doors. Lydia told her mother about Pastor Paul needing to speak with her, and that she would head home right after she met up with him. Ruth agreed, but instead of going home, she decided to stay. She wanted to give Lydia moral support, and to be there just in case Pastor Paul wanted to speak with her as well.

Abigail asked Ruth if she could wait with her, wanting to be there for Lydia too. She was more than pleased to have Abigail stay with her, knowing this would be a great time for the two of them to have a little chat themselves. And with that, the three of them headed toward the lobby.

"Don't worry, Lydia. I've prayed for your meeting with Pastor Paul," said Abigail.

Ruth encouraged her as well. "Fear not, for the Lord is always with you."

Lydia appreciated their support, but it also made her a little nervous. She didn't understand what the big deal was. Forcing herself to be brave, she turned around and headed for the hallway, leaving her mother and best friend behind in the lobby. Negative thoughts assaulted her as she walked to Pastor Paul's office.

Am I in trouble? Did I offend someone? Am I not volunteering enough? Oh, no! What if I'm being kicked out of the choir...

Lydia stopped in front of Pastor Paul's office and closed her eyes. Her blood pressure regulated as she prayed for peace and strength. Squaring her shoulders and taking in a deep breath, she knocked on the walnut grain door.

"Come in," said Pastor Paul in a loud but friendly voice.

Lydia stepped into his office and smiled. "Hey, Pastor Paul."

"Well, hello there, Lydia. So glad you could make it." His voice was more cheerful than usual. "I have some exciting news to share with you."

"Really?" Her eyes rounded with surprise.

He chuckled. "Really." He gestured to the big, comfy chair facing his desk, telling her to take a seat.

By the anxious look on her face, Pastor Paul felt bad for not telling Abigail why he wanted to speak with Lydia after service.

"My apologies, Lydia, for causing you any stress. I should have elaborated to Abigail as to why I wanted to speak with you."

A hint of pink flushed her face. "It's ok. But I'm not gonna lie...I was kinda worried until now."

There was silence for a brief moment, but then they laughed over the miscommunication.

"I don't know why I didn't think to invite Abigail." He stared at Lydia with perplexity. "She needs to hear what I have to say just as much as you do."

"I can go get her if you want me to." Lydia perked up. "She's in the lobby, with my mom."

"Oh, how wonderful!" Pastor Paul stood from his chair. "Thanks for the offer, but I'll go get them."

"Are you sure?"

He walked around his desk and patted Lydia on her shoulder. "I got this."

"Okie dokie." Lydia smiled at the possibilities of what this good news could be about.

CHAPTER 20

Pastor Paul followed Ruth and Abigail into his office. He then walked over to the bookshelf and picked up two light-weight chairs. After he placed them on either side of Lydia, he walked over to his desk and took a seat.

"I want to thank you all for coming. And I do apologize for not setting up this meeting properly. In my defense, however, I wasn't prepared for it myself." He pulled open his desk drawer and took out a folder. "Last week, I received a letter from a certain ministry."

In unison, the three of them leaned forward, their eyes fixated on the elegant envelope. He reached for a pair of glasses, next to his paperweight, and slid them on. The words **Ministry of Discovering Talents for Christ** in bold letters came into better focus. After clearing his throat, he proceeded to read the letter aloud:

Dear prospective contestant,

It's an honor and privilege to invite your church, along with others, to our 5th biennial contest. We host this event in order to give the younger generation an opportunity to be discovered for their God-given gifts and talents.

Once he finished reading the letter, he looked up at the enthralled faces staring back at him. A smile tugged at the corner of his mouth as he took off his glasses.

"The Ministry of Discovering Talents for Christ has been established for quite a while. About eight to ten years ago. And after discussing this letter with David, our worship leader, we decided that it would be very good to engage with this program once again. Over the years, we have been blessed with lots of talent in our church. Which is why we decided to be part of it—two years ago." He sat back in his chair and entwined his fingers together, seeming to reminisce. "Abigail, do you remember Rachel? The young girl who was part of the choir."

Abigail nodded. "Yeah. I do."

"I thought you would," replied Pastor Paul. "Anyhow, when we received our previous invitation, we had planned to send her to compete in the contest...Rachael had such a beautiful voice. However, it didn't go as planned. She was getting ready to leave town to attend college...." He sighed at the memory.

Lydia spoke up, telling Pastor Paul that she knew about Rachel because of Abigail. And that her story resonated with her, especially the part when she missed out on pursuing her gift of singing. But she didn't know the full story.

"And just like Rachel, you have an amazing voice too, Lydia," added Abigail.

Pastor Paul's smile reached his eyes. "Exactly! Which is why we're all here."

Lydia pulled away from his gaze, crossing her arms over her chest. She was flattered by their compliments, but she didn't want to turn beet red in front of them either. She had blushed one too many times already that day.

"Rachel was also very intelligent," continued Pastor Paul. "She had received a full scholarship from a prestigious college, and after fasting and praying, we received confirmation of what the Lord had planned for her—He wanted Rachel to pursue college. Even though she had to move to another state, we encouraged and supported her every step of the way. To this day, we've remained in contact with her parents. It brings us much joy to hear about all of the great and wondrous things He has done in Rachel's life."

When Pastor Paul expressed how significant it was for their church to receive an invitation—being the ministry had seldom sent another one out to a church who had previously received one—he created more excitement for Lydia, Ruth and Abigail.

"...their mission is to reach every church, in every state, giving everyone a chance to participate," said Pastor Paul. "Which is why it's so surprising that we received another invitation this year."

He continued to tell them about the ministry, and how the contest would be held in their state this year.

"We will always miss Rachel, but the Lord has blessed our church, and our community, with another young lady who has an exquisite voice"—Pastor Paul beamed at Lydia—"and a compassionate heart."

"Yes!" Abigail squealed and clapped her hands.

All of a sudden, Lydia felt inadequate. She was second-guessing her ability to sing, especially in front of others. Not understanding where this was coming from, she braced herself, sensing what was coming next.

"So with that said, Lydia, we would love for you to take hold of this amazing opportunity. We will do all that is necessary to see you through, making sure the contest will not interfere with your schooling, spiritual growth, and personal life. David said the contest will probably take place by the end of the summer, which shouldn't conflict with the beginning of your next school year."

Every fiber of Lydia's being tensed up.

"When the Lord presents this type of opportunity, one must feel confident along with having a peace of mind, to pursue it. And if this is what you truly want, Lydia, then you need to fan the flame of your heart," said Pastor Paul.

Abigail jumped up from her seat. "Amen to that!"

Ruth placed a hand over her chest, too stunned for words. She gave Lydia a sideways glance, her brows tugging upwards as she and her daughter gaped at one another.

"When it comes to making decisions, especially a major one such as this, you need to seek the Lord," said Pastor Paul. "In most cases, one should wait for His guidance and confirmation. However, I will need an answer by tonight or tomorrow morning. The ministry will need a response by tomorrow afternoon."

Everyone zoned in on Lydia as she sat in silence. She contemplated her love of singing and how the Lord had opened a door for her to use her voice to glorify Him. No matter how hard she tried, though, the singing contest from school still troubled her.

"Uh...am I really the one who's supposed to be competing for this event?"

"The selection for this program is based on several qualifications. And after discussing this with David, and seeking godly counsel from other members, we truly believe *you* are the one who should fulfill these requirements," replied Pastor Paul.

Abigail turned to Lydia. "I know you don't want to give up on something you've started, and I know the singing contest at school wasn't a pleasant experience. But listen to me, Lydia, this is not about winning or losing. It's about praising the Lord and singing along with like-minded individuals who want to express their love and gratitude to Him."

A tear escaped down Lydia's cheek as her fears and doubts began to lose their power over her. The words Abigail spoke were as if they were coming directly from Heaven. Everyone remained silent as a divine peace filled the space around them.

"And Lydia, if you choose to do this, you will be representing the Lord's church, shining before others, so they can see His glory," said Pastor Paul. "You will also be reaching those who do not know Him—for He wishes that no one perishes, but that all will come to repentance."

Someone knocked at the door and Pastor Paul excused himself to see who it was. When he opened it, a young woman smiled back at him. It was Hannah. She had an appointment to see him for prayer. He then turned around and introduced her to Lydia, Ruth and Abigail.

"I'm sorry, Pastor Paul. I didn't mean to interrupt," said Hannah. "I can come back another time."

"It's ok, Hannah, we were just wrapping up our time here." Pastor Paul switched his gaze over to Ruth and Lydia. "If you have any questions or concerns, just give me a call."

"We will, thank you." Ruth smiled and then she stood up. Lydia and Abigail followed suit. They made their way across the room, and right as they approached the door, Pastor Paul made one last comment.

"Again, thank you all for coming. And don't worry, Lydia. The congregation and I will keep you in our prayers as we did for Rachel."

"And we thank you, and everyone involved, for presenting this wonderful opportunity to Lydia," said Ruth.

"It is our humble pleasure. But this is all the Lord's doing," replied Pastor Paul.

A coy smile slid across Lydia's face. "Thanks, Pastor Paul. I'll give you an answer before tomorrow afternoon."

"Thank you, my dear. I hope you all have a blessed afternoon."

Everyone said their goodbyes, and then Lydia, Ruth and Abigail left his office.

On their way home, Lydia asked her mother if she and Abigail could hang out at the park for a while. She needed to be in a place where she could think, a place where peace, clarity and answers could be more within her reach. The place where she encountered two homeless men who inspired her to step out of her comfort zone, so she could encourage and help those in need.

Daniel and Joshua were the ones who had changed Lydia's perception of God, His eternal love, and who strengthened her faith in His miracles. They also reminded her of a *certain* someone who had always been there for her, shining the same light as they were. Except, Lydia was too blinded at that time to see it.

"I know the Lord can speak to us anywhere. And no matter where we are, He's always at our side. But, He also sends His angels to help us." Lydia's heart warmed as she looked over at Abigail. "Angels who don't have wings."

Abigail was at a loss for words. Her best friend had just given her the greatest compliment ever, but it was hard for her to receive it. For Abigail had felt like a complete failure after she and Lydia had their argument. All she ever wanted was to be the best friend ever, and to be a vessel of God's goodness and love. But she feared the light within had dimmed due to their conflict over the singing contest.

"Lydia, I'm beyond humbled. And I can't thank the Lord enough for you. You will always be my best friend."

Ruth teared up by the beauty and genuineness of their friendship. It made her even more grateful when she thought about the friends the Lord had blessed her with. The girls shared a few more words and then Ruth spoke up.

"Of course you can go to the park. Just make sure to be home before the sun sets, ok?"

"I will. Thanks, Mom!"

Abigail spoke next. "Thanks, Ms. Mahlon."

"You're welcome, girls. Now go seek the Lord for some answers about competing for the talent ministry."

Ruth gave Lydia a kiss on the cheek and then she kissed Abigail's. She then continued down the sidewalk as the girls crossed the street.

"I should have told you earlier, but I have to tell you about a phone call I received several weeks ago," said Lydia. "It was about the singing contest at school."

Abigail stopped in her tracks. "Say what?!"

Lydia sighed as she came to a halt, and then she turned around to face Abigail.

"Why are you just now telling me this?" asked Abigail.

"'Cause at the time, we weren't talking. And when the Lord had restored our friendship, I didn't wanna bring up the past. Especially since that experience had left such a negative impact on me—on us."

"I know where you're coming from. But this time is different. The Lord has given you a chance to use your talent according to the plan He has for you."

"I know. But I don't wanna relive what took place after the signing contest. And I don't wanna put any of my relationships at risk. You and my mom mean everything to me, and I refuse to let the enemy win again."

"And he won't. Because the Lord has your back." Abigail took a step forward. "If you still want to hang out at the park, we better get going."

"Good point."

The girls scurried down the sidewalk, making it to the park within a few minutes. No one was there, so they were able to sit on their favorite bench.

"So tell me about this phone call," said Abigail.

"Well, the results were compromised—specifically with third place. And because of that, they wanted to give me another chance to make it to nationals."

Abigail semi-froze. "Whoa."

"I know, right? I can't believe they wanted me to try out again. Who knows? I could have placed that time, going to nationals next." Lydia shook the thought out of her mind. "They were so persistent, and at one point, I almost caved in."

Abigail closed her eyes and pushed out a relieved breath. "It's so much harder to do what is right than to give in to our flesh. Or to give in to the desires of others.

But I'm so proud of you for standing your ground. Like the Bible says, 'Greater is he who is in us than he who is in the world.' And don't despair, because the Lord will greatly bless you for rejecting their offer."

"Thanks for the encouragement."

Abigail smiled. "Anytime."

"Some days, I struggle with regrets—the *what ifs* and *could haves*. Winning the contest, and using the money to support my mom, still appeals to me. Not like it used to, though. The thought of being famous, or at least being in the lime light for a short while, kinda excites me too."

"I appreciate your honesty. And believe it or not, I've been there too. We all have. When the enemy takes our desires and dangles them in front of us, giving us the chance to take hold of them, it's hard to resist the temptation."

Abigail reached in the pocket of her jeans and took out her phone. Lydia watched as she searched through her Bible app.

"Here's a Scripture that goes along with what we're talking about, 'The flesh is weak, but the spirit is willing.'" She continued to search through her app. "And here's one in the book of Matthew that talks about talent...."

Abigail slid her phone back in her pocket and then shifted her position to face Lydia.

"Everyone has talent, Lydia. But there are many who never put them to use. And if they do, they don't always use them according to the Lord's purposes. I know how determined you are, so please don't let the past discourage you from pursuing this amazing opportunity the Lord has given you. I'd hate to see you hide your talent just like the unwise servant did."

Lydia's countenance radiated with understanding as everything began to take shape. She looked straight ahead as if envisioning what it would be like if she were to accept the Lord's call. A burning passion rose within her, and she wanted nothing more than to proclaim how good He was, including all that He had done for her and her mother.

"Wow! What an eye-opener." Lydia threw her arms around Abigail. "I've made up my mind—I'm going for it!"

CHAPTER 21

Lydia and Abigail walked past the Sunday school classes, but then they stopped in the middle of the hallway to pray.

"Father, I ask you to remove any kind of hindrance that will prevent Lydia from using the talent you have given her. And please use her voice to shine for those who are still in darkness. Thank you, Father, for hearing my prayer. In Jesus's wonderful name I pray. Amen," said Abigail.

"Amen," echoed Lydia. "Thanks so much for the prayers, Abby."

"But of course."

They hugged each other and then proceeded to Pastor Paul's office. He opened the door after the first knock, and invited them to step inside. Like a child on Christmas

Day, he fidgeted with excitement, wondering what Lydia's answer would be. A moment later, he jumped up for joy when she told him she wanted to participate in the contest.

He thanked her for accepting the opportunity, and then asked if she could see how the Lord had intervened concerning the first singing contest. And then he mentioned that if she had qualified, then she wouldn't be getting ready to make preparations in order to compete in the Ministry of Discovering Talents for Christ.

Before the girls had left, he prayed over Lydia for protection, guidance, and support. And then he took out his cell phone to share the wonderful news with David.

"Lydia, can I ask you something?" said Ruth.

"Sure. What is it, Mom?"

"If you had made it in the National Singing Contest, and reached where you wanted to be, do you think we would be where we are right now?"

"Wow! That's exactly what Pastor Paul had asked me." Lydia brightened, excited by their conversation. "And to answer your question—I don't think so."

"Me either. It was very possible you could have won the competition, and we could have been better off financially. But finding God and receiving His eternal salvation, may not have ever happened. If we could do it all over again, I wouldn't change a thing. God is the source of everything good. And no one, or anything, can ever compare to Him. Not only that, but He healed me!"

"I couldn't have said it better myself!" Lydia gave her mother a high-five.

"My, you're pretty strong." Ruth giggled. "But anyways, I didn't mean to bring up the past to make you feel bad. I just wanted you to reflect, hoping you would see how the Lord redeemed your heart's desire and gave you something way better—another chance to use your talent to bless Him and others. Plus, I'm sure there will be more blessings along the path He has set before you to follow."

"No apologies needed, Mom. We definitely needed to talk about this, so we can appreciate His mercy, grace and salvation."

"I'm so proud of you, honey."

"And I'm just as proud of you, Mom."

"Remember, as long as you do your part, always giving it your best, God will do the rest."

It had been a few days since Lydia started practicing with David. And during this time, he sought the Lord as to what songs she should sing—they were both ecstatic when He had revealed the song choices. David was amazed by her dedication to their practice sessions. For Lydia had been showing up before he did, every single time. He was also impressed by her outstanding vocals and the great range she displayed. Lydia had amazing control and hardly missed a beat.

"Lydia, do you have any musical background?" asked David.

"No. But I have been singing since a very young age."

He arched a brow. "Really?"

"Yeah. Why?"

"Because I've been training a number of choir members in our church, including others, but it's surprising to see you perform like a professional singer."

"Wow…thanks."

"If you don't mind, may I ask how old you are?"

"I'll be eighteen in October."

"Well, for someone your age, you have such a mature voice. Your techniques are spot on, and the way you engage with an audience, makes you a perfect contender."

Lydia beamed. "Despite the lack of training, I've performed quite a bit throughout the years. The most recent time I did was during The National Singing Contest, which was sponsored by our high school."

Lydia continued to tell David about her experience with the singing contest, and how she had missed the cut by coming in at fourth place. She then told him about the phone call she had received over the summer, and how the judges wanted to give her another chance to try out due to the scores being comprised. And how she had been originally chosen for third place.

David was captivated by her story, and as she continued to speak, he crossed his arms over his chest, leaning his back against the wall.

"We had a coach, but it was more like having a volunteer. Don't get me wrong, he had a really good voice and knew a lot about singing, but he wasn't a trained professional."

"Hm? I wonder the reason as to why they weren't prepared. Better said, more professional about it. After all, you guys were going to represent your school on a national level."

"I'm guessing it was a resource issue. I'm not trying to blame anyone, but I agree with you. They should have put more effort into our preparation. Whether we had vocal coaches or not, our passion for singing is what kept us going. We worked with what we had, what we knew to do, you know what I mean?"

David nodded. "So I'm assuming you never took them up on their offer to audition again, right?"

"Right. But it all worked out for the best, though. My mom was very sick during that time, and since I didn't make the cut, I had more time to take care of her. A lot happened during the summer, but the best part was getting to know the Lord...."

Lydia talked about when she and her mother had given their lives to Christ, and how He had healed her mother of cancer.

"...after being a born-again Christian, I've realized that getting to the top of the world isn't worth it. Anything it has to offer will never compare to the peace, joy, and meaningful life I have now."

David was stunned. "Whoa...that's one remarkable testimony. Turning down the possibility of riches to support your mother and yourself along with fame—was no easy feat, I'm sure. I don't even know if I would trust myself to do what you did. I really don't." He paused. "Thanks for sharing your story, Lydia. You have taught me a very important lesson of doing what is right in the sight of the Lord."

"You're welcome." Lydia smiled. "It's my mission to give godly advice. Paying it forward, you know? I have a best friend who has always tried to steer me in the right direction, including two homeless men the Lord had sent my way."

David stepped away from the wall. "I think this will be enough for today. We'll resume practice tomorrow—same place, same time."

"Ok, sounds great."

"But before you leave, can you give this to Grace? It's next week's schedule and she needs to look over it."

"Sure. No problem." Lydia took it from him and then she left.

David, however, stayed behind to arrange some stuff in the room. When he had finished, he sat down and took out an envelope from his back pocket. It was a contract he was about to seal with some musicians who played secular music. His plan was to train them as vocalists. As he stared at it, he became deeply convicted and dropped the envelope.

He knelt on his knee, bowed his head, and then closed his eyes.

"Father God, thank you for showing me your mercy, and for teaching me something great through Lydia's testimony. I have been honoring you with my lips, but my heart has been far from your presence. Please, Lord, help me to live a righteous and authentic life...."

Lydia woke up early Friday morning, feeling very excited and nervous. After days of relentless practice, the day had finally arrived—the day of the contest. She knelt down bedside her bed and prayed.

"Heavenly Father, who am I that you are mindful of me, bringing me this far? I thank you so much for blessing me with a voice to praise and glorify you. Father, please give me a spirit of peace and strength as I perform today. And allow me to showcase your glory by manifesting your wonderful name to the judges, to the audience, and to my fellow competitors. Help me to rejoice with the winner and not to covet. Let your will be done, not mine. I pray this in your name above all names...amen."

Ruth was about to knock on Lydia's door, but she heard her speaking to the Lord. So she waited a few seconds to knock again.

"Come in," called Lydia.

"Hey, honey, today's the big day. How are you feeling?"

"Better than before." Lydia stood up. "I was on the verge of freaking out, but then I prayed."

"Don't worry, honey, the Lord will get you through the day. He is faithful and will never fail us."

Lydia exhaled. "I know. But there's always a constant battle between my faith and flesh. Like a little devil on one shoulder, and a little angel on the other."

A sympathetic smile slid across Ruth's face. "No matter one's spiritual level, I'm positive this is something all Christians struggle with. And remember, no matter the outcome, it's a blessing for all of us to be a part of this God-orchestrated event."

"Thanks, Mom, for reminding me of what truly matters."

"Of course, honey. And thank you for doing the same for me." She walked over to Lydia and gently took her arm. "Come on, let's get ready."

CHAPTER 22

Lydia's phone rang. "Hi David. Yeah, I'm ok. How about you?"

"Same here," replied David. "So, you ready for the big day?"

"By the Lord's grace and my mom's support—I am."

"Wonderful. I'll be at your house by 11:30 a.m. We need to head out as early as possible to avoid rush-hour."

"Ok. See ya then!" Lydia ended the call and turned around. "Mom, David will be here in about half an hour."

"We better hurry up and eat then."

"Eat?"

"Yes, I made us lunch. You need your strength before the contest. We both do."

"*Ugh...fine.*"

"But where's Abigail? She should have been here already."

"She's on her way."

"I hope so because I made lunch for her too."

Abigail finally arrived and the three of them rushed through their early lunch. As they cleared the table, the doorbell rang. It was David. Everyone was excited but overwhelmed at the same time. Before they left the house, David led them in prayer, asking for protection, peace, strength, and for the Lord's purposes to be accomplished concerning the outcome of the contest.

They drove for an hour, and then they arrived at the convention center, which was located downtown. Lydia's heart began to race as they entered the building in a small huddle. Ruth and Abigail didn't want to leave her, but family members, friends, and anyone who came to support the contestants were not allowed backstage. So before they headed to the auditorium, they spoke words of peace and comfort over her along with Scriptures concerning her self-worth and value, reminding Lydia about her true identity in Christ. For no man, no circumstance, and no contest could ever diminish or take that away from her. They also reminded her that all of God's children are priceless and perfect in His sight. Lydia teared up as they parted ways, feeling grateful to have such a loving mother and best friend.

David guided Lydia through a corridor, which led them to the area where they were checking in all the contestants. As far as the procedure was concerned, it was nothing new to Lydia. For she had a similar experience when she auditioned for the singing contest earlier that summer. The only difference was the size of the building and the amount of people who filled it.

Once Lydia was checked in, she watched some of the contestants, who had arrived earlier, rehearsing backstage along with their trainers. David, however, had to gently pull her away, telling her it was time for her to practice as well. He had found a spot that was a little bit quieter, and as she rehearsed, a few people gathered nearby. She didn't notice them at first, but when she did, she lowered her voice. Still, her beautiful singing was loud enough to attract others. Some were contestants and the others were trainers. A few staff members had stopped to listen as well.

An announcement had made its way backstage, letting the contestants know to take their positions. The small crowd that had gathered to hear Lydia sing, quickly broke apart and headed to the assigned room. David and Lydia trailed behind.

The contest had begun. And the eight finalists who had been chosen to represent their churches, took the stage, one by one. Lydia was amazed by all the talent, but it also made her nervous. Her fears increased by the way the crowd had cheered and applauded after each performance. She started to doubt if she was good enough to be among her fellow contestants, not knowing who to be more afraid of: the crowd or the judges. For each contestant was judged and critiqued, in great detail, immediately after.

This was it—it was time for Lydia to perform. Ruth and Abigail joined hands when they saw her walking across the stage. She introduced herself, saying where she was from, and which church she was representing. One of the judges asked her what she was going to be singing, and "Merciful Redemption" was Lydia's response.

When Lydia sang, everyone in the auditorium was mesmerized by her beautiful voice. But it was also the song she had chosen to sing, which resonated with many. All in all, it was the connection she had made with the audience that won them over.

After she finished her performance, Ruth and Abigail jumped to their feet, cheering for her at the top of their lungs. And then, the unexpected happen—everyone else joined in, giving Lydia a standing ovation. The judges included.

They remained on their feet, applauding and cheering, a few seconds longer before the judges took over.

"Wow," said the first judge. "That was absolutely incredible."

"You performed in such a heartfelt and authentic way," added the second judge.

The third judge grinned from ear to ear. "Your vocals are flawless...."

"Agreed," said the first judge. "Your performance was so outstanding that I have to ask—is this your first time on stage?"

Lydia shook her head. "No, it isn't. I tried out for the National Singing Contest a few months ago."

"Still, only after two performances, your skills and stage presence are amazing," concluded the first judge.

Lydia smiled. "Thank you."

"If you don't mind, will you please tell us about the first contest," began the second judge. "It would be great to hear about your experience, the process, and anything else you'd like to share with us."

"First of all, it was a non-Christian signing contest. And after the first audition, I was selected to represent my high school. But when I finally competed, I made fourth place. I was really upset because I wanted to win, in order to help my mom with her medical bills and treatments."

"So you tried out in hopes of helping your sick mother," stated the third judge.

"Yes. And just to support the both of us in general. My mom was sick for a long time and she wasn't able to work."

Compassion and admiration appeared on the judge's face, including the other two. Murmurs and whispers of respect along with a myriad of teary eyes transpired from the audience as well. They were all inspired and encouraged by Lydia's love, selflessness and humility.

"Praise the Lord for His love and goodness." The second judge wiped away the tears from her face.

The first judge sniffled. "Amen to that."

"Lydia, we have one last question for you," said the third judge. "But please know there is no judgement attached to it."

Lydia stiffened. "Ok."

"Why did you try out for a secular contest?" asked the third judge.

"Because I wasn't born again at the time." She bowed her head and closed her eyes, feeling overwhelmed by all the hardships she and her mother had endured. Lifting up her head, she continued, "But my best friend was, and she always encouraged me with God's Word along with pointing me in the right direction."

Ruth and Abigail held each other as the tears continued to flow. Without Lydia speaking another word, they could feel what was in her heart.

"But I was too stubborn to take my best friend's advice about the contest, especially when she talked to me about God and my eternal welfare." Lydia steadied her breathing and then continued, "It was because of my best friend, and a special group of people, that I finally sought the Lord and gave my life to Him. The best part—my mom did too."

Lydia felt led to go a little further, so she told the judges about her mother's miraculous recovery. She also told them about wanting to experience the fame that went along with winning the National Singing Contest. But that her desires, morals and priorities had been set straight because of the Lord's conviction through her best friend's continual warnings of seeking the world's way for success.

Almost forgetting why she was on stage, the judges thanked Lydia for answering all of their questions along with sharing her testimony. They also told her that they were ready to critique her performance.

Lydia's body tingled with nerves, but the Holy Ghost wrapped His peace around her like a warm, cozy blanket.

"Your overall performance was great. You engaged with the audience, your song of choice was perfect, and so was your vocal quality and projection," said the first judge. "Everything, and I mean everything, was spot on."

The audience applauded and Lydia felt relieved.

"Thank you." Lydia smiled.

The second judge commented next. "Lydia, you have one of the most beautiful and powerful voices I've ever heard. But what impressed me the most—was your testimony. Your voice, including what you've been through, will no doubt make it to the top of the charts nationwide."

Lydia was blown away. "Wow. Talk about being humbled. Thank you so much."

This made everyone smile.

"We are always searching for the next big star," began the third judge. A certain someone to proclaim the name of the Lord, bringing hope and truth to others through anointed songs and music." He cleared his throat and took a sip of water. "I have nothing else to say. Because you, Lydia, have left me speechless." His eyes twinkled as he looked up at her.

The judges thanked Lydia for her performance, and for giving her testimony, one last time. A round of applause from the audience, and the judges, accompanied her as she walked off the stage.

CHAPTER 23

The results were in, and the host of the contest spoke into the microphone, calling each contestant onto the stage, in the order they had performed. Lydia was the last one to be called upon. Faint chatting filled the auditorium as the judges took their seats once again.

They huddled together and spoke in hush tones. Seconds later, the judges waved the host over. He walked across the stage and then down the steps, making his way to the judges' panel. One of the judges handed him a golden envelope, and as he walked back onto the stage, anticipation loomed from the contestants as they waited for the final results.

Lydia's heart pounded violently as she watched the envelope being opened in what seemed to be slow motion. Her nervousness intensified and she began to hyperventilate. But then the Holy Ghost swept away all of her fear and infused her with His peace and strength.

The host leaned into the microphone, holding a piece of paper. Lydia closed her eyes and rested in His presence.

"Before I announce the winner, please give a big round of applause for all the contestants, their families, and the churches they are representing."

Lydia opened her eyes and blew out a sigh of relief, feeling grateful for another moment of ease before the big announcement.

"And now for the moment we have all been waiting for." The host paused for dramatic effect. "The winner for this year's contest is...Lydia Mahlon!"

With a stunned gaze, Lydia blinked and then shook her head, wondering if she had imagined her name being called out or not. The audience stood once again, expressing their enthusiasm and delight, as they honored Lydia with thundering shouts and praises. Ruth and Abigail jumped for joy, their arms flailing above their heads.

The host asked Lydia to come forward, but she was in a state of shock, not sure if she could move. Somehow, someway, she began moving toward the front of the stage, feeling as if a cluster of clouds were carrying her.

The host beamed as he draped a golden sash over Lydia along with handing her a glimmering first-place trophy. He gently took her right arm and raised it up with his. "It is an honor to present Lydia Mahlon as this year's winner of The Biennial Christian Gospel Music Contest!"

Overcome with an array of positive emotions, all Lydia could do was stand there and smile as tears gushed down her face.

"Congratulations, Lydia. Can you please tell us what's going through your mind right now?"

"God is real. And His loving-kindnesses and tender mercies are overwhelming." Lydia sucked in a breath. "With God, all things are possible. Trust me, me and mom are living proof."

Repeated "amens" echoed throughout the auditorium.

"It is so humbling and such an honor to be on this stage—first-place winner or not," said Lydia.

Lydia searched the first three rows, knowing her mother and best friend were standing somewhere in the midst of all the exuberant and happy faces. Finally, she had spotted them.

"Mom! Will you wave your hands above your head, so everyone can see you?"

Ruth glowed with a brilliant light as acclamation broke out on her behalf.

"Now it's my best friend's turn." Lydia beamed "Abigail, show yourself!"

Abigail turned bright red as she waved a shaky arm above her head. She had always been on the reserved and introverted side, but the upbeat acknowledgement filled her with confidence and gladness. Ruth and Abigail joined hands, raising them one last time, before the audience had settled down.

Lydia pulled away from the microphone and asked if she could continue speaking. The host nodded his approval and took a step back.

"I thank all of you for supporting me tonight, including the pastor and worship leader of our church. Pastor Paul and David—wherever you are, please make yourselves known! The both of you deserve recognition too."

Pastor Paul and David emerged from the right-hand side of the stage. With illuminated countenances, they walked toward Lydia. She gave them a hug and then thanked them for their compassion, prayers, and all the support they had given to her and her mother. As she continued to speak, they remained at her side.

"I never thought I'd have the opportunity to perform on stage again. My passion has always been singing, but over the summer, my eyes and heart had been opened to what truly matters." Lydia paused. "My best friend Abigail had prayed for me and my mom, day and night, making us her joy and crown before the Lord. And even though my mom had cancer, she remained steadfast throughout it all. She's the strongest and bravest woman I know."

Ruth and Abigail embraced one another as they sat in utter meekness and gratitude.

"I also wanna acknowledge two very special men who greatly inspired me through their testimonies. They gave me hope to trust in the Lord's unfailing love and His healing hands. And they also motivated me to start reading the Bible."

"Hallelujah! Praise the Lord!" a couple of men shouted.

Everyone turned their heads, gaping at the two men who stood in the audience. Lydia squinted to see who it was, and when they came into focus, her eyes widened and her mouth fell agape. Daniel and Joshua stood three rows up from Ruth and Abigail.

"There is no better reward than to witness the testimony of those the Lord has sent our way!" said Daniel.

"Seeing how the Lord has intervened in your life, including your mother's, testifies the goodness and faithfulness of our Lord!" added Joshua. "We are greatly encouraged and we pray that everyone here will be too."

"Lydia, you truly deserve to be recognized for being faithful to the Lord. You have endured every season, every trial, so be assured that you will receive your rewards from God," said Daniel. "We speak on behalf of your best friend too!"

And with that, the two men had left. Lydia desperately wanted to thank them in person, but all she could see was the back of their shirts as they headed toward the exit.

Ruth and Abigail stayed close to one another as they made their way through the crowd, trying to get to the stage. They jogged up the steps and rushed toward Lydia with open arms.

"I'm so proud of you, baby girl!" cried Ruth.

"Me too!" said Abigail. "I told you the Lord had a wonderful plan for you and your amazing voice."

Lydia gave them the tightest squeeze ever. "I'm so proud of you, too, Mom! And Abigail, I can't wait to see what awesome plans the Lord has in store for you!"

They savored the precious moment a little longer before the host came and told Ruth that the judges wanted to speak with her. Lydia and Abigail remained in the same spot, and as Abigail continued to talk, Lydia scanned the auditorium, hoping Daniel and Joshua had returned.

"Abigail, did you tell them I'd be here?"

"Who are you talking about?"

"Daniel and Joshua."

"No. But I was wondering the same thing."

"Then how did they know where to find me?" Lydia was very perplexed. "Anyways, I really wanted to talk with them, but they left in such a hurry."

"Yeah, I wonder why?" Abigail scratched her head. "Maybe they had to—"

"Wait...is that?"—Lydia stood on her toes, looking over Abigail's head—"I think I see them standing by the exit."

Abigail quirked a brow. "Say what?"

Lydia grabbed her arm. "Come on, Abby, let's get to them before they leave again."

The girls rushed over to Ruth and apologized for interrupting her conversation with the judges. Lydia told her they would be right back and asked if she could hold on to her trophy. Ruth took the trophy, and then she told them not to take too long, and to be careful.

As the girls maneuvered through the crowd, several people had asked Lydia for her autograph and picture. And with much grace, Lydia told them she needed a few minutes to herself, but that she would return to do so. Wasting no time, they continued toward the exit, but when they got there, Daniel and Joshua were nowhere in sight.

"Oh, no! We're too late." Lydia pouted as they came to a halt. "Who knows where they could have gone now?"

"I'm sorry, Lydia." Abigail wrapped an arm around her shoulder. "Don't be so hard on yourself, though. After all, nobody can chase angels—unless they have wings too."

Lydia beamed. "So you really think..."

"Oh, come on! How many more miracles will it take to fully convince you when it comes to the supernatural?" Abigail grinned.

They stared at each other for a moment, and then they busted out laughing.

"Fair enough," replied Lydia.

They linked arms and made their way back to the stage. There was so much to rejoice over, but the greatest gift of all, was God's merciful redemption.

EPILOGUE

Lydia was showcased on the main page of the Christian Gospel Music Contest website along with being invited to numerous major events. A few months later, Lydia released her first album. She started touring throughout different cities and states, including other countries around the world.

And through it all, Lydia and Abigail had concentrated on their education, they even got accepted to the same college the following year. Sometime later, Ruth went back to her doctor for a checkup. She was told that she still had no signs and symptoms of the disease, and that she was cancer-free—for good.

Matthew 25:14-30 (KJV)